2121

2121

David Railey

2121

iUniverse books may be ordered through booksellers or by contacting:

iUniverse
1663 Liberty Drive
Bloomington, IN 47403
www.iuniverse.com
1-800-Authors (1-800-288-4677)

ISBN: 978-1-5320-4514-1 (sc)
ISBN: 978-1-5320-4513-4 (e)

Library of Congress Control Number: 2018904565

Print information available on the last page.

iUniverse rev. date: 04/17/2018

AUTHOR'S NOTES

Pronunciation Guide for Character's Chinese Names

The authentic character names used in "2121," are in "Pinyin" – the Romanized alphabet of Mandarin. Many of the vowels and consonants are *not* pronounced the way they are in the English alphabet.

Zhou Xingjia – her family name is Zhou (what we call a last name), her given name is Xingjia (what we call a first name). Zhou is pronounced "Joe", Xingjia is pronounced "Shing-gee-ah."

Mr. Zhou – (Xingjia's father) Zhou is pronounced the same as above, i.e. "Joe"

Huang Bei – his family name is Huang, his chosen/given name is Bei. Huang is pronounced "Whang," like the wha in "what," and Bei is pronounced "Bay."

Dr. Chen Wu Chen – his family name is Chen, and his given name is Wu Chen. The "e" in Chen is like the name Ben, i.e. Chen rhymes with Ben. The "u" in Wu sounds like a cow's "moo."

Mei – Xingjia's friend's first name or given name, is pronounced "May."

Li Jian – his family name is Li, and his given name is Jian. Li is pronounced "Lee," and Jian is pronounced "Gee-an."

Zhang Wei – (briefly introduced in the bar scene) his family name is Zhang, and his given name is Wei. Zhang is pronounced like the name John with a "g" on the end "Johng," and Wei is pronounce "Way."

Huang Long – his family name is Huang, and his given name is Long. Huang, already mentioned – is pronounced "Whang," and Long is just like you would pronounce it in English, like the word long instead of short.

Li Quing – her family name is Li, and her given name in Quing. Li is pronounced "Lee," and Quing is pronounced "Ching."

Shen Bo – his family name is Shen, and his given name is Bo. Shen is pronounced "shin," and Bo just like it would be in English with a long o.

Li Na – her family name is Li, and Na is her given name. Li is pronounced "Lee," and Na is pronounced "Nah."

Huang Ming – her family name is Huang, and her given name is Ming. Huang is "Whang," as previously listed, and Ming is pronounced like it would be in English, i.e. rhymes with "sing."

Huang Ling – his family name is Huang, and his given name is Ling. Huang is listed several times and is the family name of all 4 related *companions*. "Ling" rhymes with Ming.

Wang He – (Ming's boyfriend) his family name is Wang, and his given name is He. Wang is pronounced with a soft "a" like the "a" in "what," and He is pronounced like "Hu," the "e" has a "u" sound as in "uh."

CONTENTS

CHAPTER ONE

BEFORE

Zhou Xingjia gazed out the large 70th floor office window that offered a nearly panoramic view of Beijing. Xingjia's grandmother had told her that Beijing had changed so much in her own life, that she could never have believed it would change even more, but it did. Even 70-stories up, there were shadows from much taller buildings. The view faced west, still the College side of the city, the realm of universities and academia. Xingjia could see the Peking University Tower that had been erected in 2100, a now famous steel landmark 54-stories high - with an exterior that gave one the impression of the Great Wall in a modern spiral. From a distance, it looked like a giant screw pointing at the sky, inspiring local names that implied something else. Her first boyfriend in college had worn a t-shirt with a screen picture of "*the* tower" on it, along with the word "SCREW" boldly printed underneath. She had hated that t-shirt, but she loved Tian. She loved Tian the way one falls in love in college, with parents finally absent, eating a bad diet, awake into the wee hours, feeling his hands on her skin beneath her shirt. She remembered the intensity of his eyes, his reassuring smile, and his laugh. Being with Tian was easy in college. They shared mutual friends. There was no pressure.

After college, she thought, her jaw tightening, *that's when the pressure started. Maybe the buildings are taller now, and there's 40-million people in Beijing instead of the 20-million of a century ago, but some things never change,* she said to herself. Even in 2121 parents in China still expected their children to get married after college as soon as possible, and start a family right away. Things had not worked that way for Xingjia. She had majored in business and finance, but following graduation, she had burned-out after two years in mergers and acquisitions. Her social life had been even worse. The men she worked with were lewd pigs, constantly making offensive sexual references and pushing for sex on the first date. Her boss had made advances early-on, and her rejection of his advances and report of his inappropriate behavior had made her job even more stressful. Xingjia didn't fit in and she knew it, though she had tried to make it work. She was well aware that she *looked* younger than her age, and that men seemed to assume she was naïve. In addition she was an original beauty, with sensuous lips and mischievous eyes, offset by a sprinkling of freckles on her face – an uncommon feature among Chinese people. Of medium height, she had a perfect figure and looked good in anything she wore – but she wished she was taller, and she didn't like her freckles and complained to her own reflection in the mirror that her eyes were too wide apart and strange looking. Of course, she knew guys were attracted to her, but she found most of them boring. Her quick original comebacks tended to unnerve all but the smartest guys, and even these she could easily confuse, her favored defensive tactic. Despite her long hours, she did her best to leave time for dating, but dating was like a job interview, except both people were interviewing for the same job. Xingjia's life was not what she had imagined it would be.

She quit her job and took a 3-month sabbatical, announcing to her parents that she wanted to go back to college and major in AstroPsychology. Her parents were not pleased. They had no objection to AstroPsychology, which had become a lucrative, growing field, with many career opportunities, especially in the android industry. What her parents objected to was the loss of time. "You'll be twenty-six by the time you get another degree. Is postponing marriage and family *that long* a risk you're prepared to take?" her father had plainly stated. "Your chances for marriage decrease after twenty-seven," her mother added, "and go down with every year that follows." However, no argument could dissuade her, so reluctantly her parents agreed to foot the bill one more time for her college education.

She dove into her studies, excelling academically. She had found her passion in AstroPsychology. It even made dating more interesting. Now when she was on a date she could use what she was learning in AstroPsychology to explore more about the other person and even reveal more about herself. Still, almost nothing clicked. The one guy she really liked turned out to have a wife in Xiamen, which he managed to mention 6-months into the relationship. She knew she should've ended the relationship right then, but she let it drag on for 3-more months. She had learned in her studies to recognize relationship patterns, and it was obvious to her that she was somehow managing to avoid finding a relationship that had a potential for marriage and family. In addition, she had begun to question whether she actually wanted to get married and have a family. Some weeks she wanted to and some weeks she didn't. After she graduated and got an excellent position with BHAI, the pressure from her parents to get married and start a family became nearly intolerable. She didn't even want to visit them, because the subject of marriage was *always* the main topic!

Xingjia wanted to please her parents. Yet, she hated the ancient haunting saying of "the eyes of a parent without grandchildren remain open beyond death." Her own parents had mellowed into a peaceful older couple. She refused to say "elderly." However, things were not always so peaceful. She remembered them arguing and fighting when she grew-up. She especially remembered hearing her mother loudly sobbing alone one night, when her father was away on business. She had lay in bed listening, wondering what was wrong. Courageously for a nine-year-old girl she slipped out of bed to find out. Sitting next to her mom, her mother had held her closely – her pajamas wet with tears. "Men are different, darling." They don't understand women at all. Your father can't help it, he's just a man after all." Xingjia could not fathom what could make men and women so different. She knew boys were different physically, and they seemed a bit slow or dumb sometimes in figuring out what she and her girlfriends could tell right away. But she couldn't connect her mother's tears with anything she knew at nine. She was aware of that her mother's sadness, and assumed this had something to do with her father's work requiring he be away from home nearly half the time. For Xingjia her father would always bring her little gifts when he came home, and something for her mom as well. Over time her parents bickered less and less. "A normal couple; a normal family, I suppose," she had thought.

Nonetheless, her studies in AstroPsychology had led her to examine her family dynamics. Whenever she was back home on weekends or holidays she used her private time with her mom to discuss the past and explore her mother's experiences. At first her mother had been resistant to revisit anything painful from her past, but gradually her mom opened-up. Xingjia learned that at that time when she was nine and had heard her mother sobbing, that her mother had discovered Xingjia's father was having an affair that had been going on for several years. So it was, that during the period that Xingjia was back in college majoring in AstroPsychology, she grew closer to her mother during these visits. Xingjia could still feel her mother's pain, and she considered how her mother's pain and disappointments had influenced her own development. Synchronistically, she had learned of her father's long ago affair during the same time that she was dating the married man. Such ironic parallels were important and meaningful in AstroPsychology, and she grew in her understanding of her past and of herself.

Unfortunately for Xingjia, graduation had ended those weekend discussions with her Mom, and any conversation now always returned to "getting married and starting a family." Her work at the Beijing Holistic Artificial Intelligence (BHAI) corporation, had proved to be very engaging and stimulating. It was both another world and the "new" world, and everything was changing in ways that even the best forecasters were unsure of how to predict. As it was, no one had predicted what had already happened. Xingjia had studied the history of western astrology in the 20th Century and its growth in China during the early decades of the 21st Century. She knew how astrology had reinvented itself on a timeline that paralleled developments in psychology. Both Humanistic and Transpersonal psychology had influenced the emergence of Humanistic Astrology, leading to Archetypal Astrology, Evolutionary Astrology, and Astropsychology. Yet it seemed that these new branches of astrology would remain "alternative counseling methodologies," only respected by a few in academia – and while serving millions who consulting these modern astrologers to understand themselves better and create a more fulfilling life, still ignored or denounced by mainstream science.

Then a most unexpected thing occurred. Dr. Chen Wu Chen, an AI developer for Beijing Artificial Intelligence (BAI), the corporate predecessor to BHAI – the "H" for Holistic would be inserted later because of Dr. Chen, decided to turn the focus of his genius upon *astrology*. Dr. Chen had already accomplished more in the development of Artificial Intelligence and android design than anyone thought possible, but he had reached a dead end. Already science had successfully advanced robotics and android development to such a level of task performance that robots and androids had

5

become an indispensable part of modern society. However, Dr. Chen and his team were attempting to find a way to take androids to an unprecedented level of sophistication, a level of interaction with human beings that would satisfy the intrinsic social needs of being human. "Imagine an android as a friend, your best friend, a member of your family, your companion – perhaps a lifelong companion," he had stated at the outset of his project. "I'm not talking about a *pet*, but someone you experience as an equal – who is there for you whenever you need them."

There were some that thought this went too far, that if it could be done it would undermine the social fabric of society. Many at BAI thought the investment of resources into this project was a waste of time and money. However, Dr. Chen was convinced it could be and should be done, and that humanity would be richer for it. The only problem was he could not find the right psychological model upon which to base his design. Every psychological model failed to match or even come close to the intricately nuanced essence of human interaction. Physically, the best androids already "felt real," warm smooth skin that was pleasant to touch, even a hand to hold for children with android nannies, nurses in hospitals, caregivers for the elderly, and – yes, even female or male "prostitute androids" – whose level of "realness" depended on the price tag. The government had originally tried to ban prostitute androids, but had acquiesced to strict control of sales, user fees, and safety regulations. Yet even the most expensive prostitute androids, were still androids with a robotic nonhuman quality. Despite an erotic android subculture expressed through pop songs, art, film, and even poetry – all was projection. One knew instantly without hesitation or doubt that they were using a not-human device.

Dr. Chen was looking for an enhanced holistic operating system that would fractalize messaging creatively through its synthetic neural network, allowing for the right mix of sensory input, self-awareness, and simultaneous responsiveness and interaction. Memory, along with a self-correcting learning process was already a well-developed feature of android products. People depended upon the logical and precisely calculated information that androids could provide. An android nurse could continually monitor vital signs, administer medication, keep a detailed medical history, provide up-to-the-minute reports upon demand, and offer the solace of "touch" to patients. Yet even these valuable health care androids, were still medical devices, and only children imagined they were more.

Dr. Chen imagined they could be more as well, and after rapidly accessing nearly every academically archived article and text on holistic systems he came across a reference to astrology that gave him a chilled pause. He found it in the work of a controversial 20th Century psychiatrist, named Stanislov Grof, who had spent five decades researching non-ordinary states of consciousness. Working with psychiatric patients and LSD in the 1960's, Grof found patterns of similarity in both the non-ordinary states of consciousness of his patients and others that had taken LSD under careful supervision. Stan Grof also grew to believe that these non-ordinary states of consciousness actually resonated with the human birth process. He identified four stages of Perinatal Experience, which he called BPM, for Birth Perinatal Matrix. All of this was interesting enough, but it was this passage from an article written in 2005, that caught Dr. Chen's attention, especially the sentences Dr. Chen highlighted below:

The effort to discover a method for predicting the reaction to psychedelics and the therapeutic outcome was one of the objectives of a large clinical study that our research team conducted at the Maryland Psychiatric Research Center in the 1960s and 1970s. We used for this purpose a battery of standard psychological tests,

including the Minnesota Multidimensional Personality Inventory (MMPI), Shostrom's Personal Orientation Inventory (POI), the Rorschach Inkblot Test, our own Psychedelic Experience Questionnaire (PEQ), and others. This research confirmed my earlier findings at the Psychiatric Research Institute in Prague, Czechoslovakia, and the conclusion from the study of professional literature, that the results of the tests developed and commonly used by Western psychology were essentially useless in this regard. Ironically, when after years of frustrating effort, I finally found a tool that made such predictions possible, it was more controversial than psychedelics themselves. It was astrology, a discipline that, even after years of studying transpersonal phenomena, I myself tended to dismiss as a ridiculous pseudoscience. I came to realize, however, that astrology could be an invaluable tool in the work with both psychedelics and with other forms of non-ordinary (or "holotropic") states of consciousness such as those induced by powerful experiential techniques of psychotherapy (primal therapy, rebirthing, and holotropic breathwork) or occurring spontaneously during psychospiritual crises.

Dr. Chen immediately saw a parallel between his own frustration in finding a workable psychological model upon which to pattern the equations of his design, and the very similar frustration Grof expressed. But, Astrology?!

Over the next 6-months, Dr. Chen devoured everything he could find on astrology, and met secretly once a week with a semi-retired professional astrologer for lessons. Always the prodigy, Chen both astonished and alarmed his elderly tutor with the speed of his progress and comprehension. Kindly but firmly admonished that it takes years to learn how to apply and practice astrology, Chen reassured his teacher that his interests were as a scientist only, that he had no intention of practicing the profession. Fascinated by the holistic matrix of astrology, as a scientist Chen examined astrology from every point of analysis, especially as a mathematical model. Later Dr. Chen would write, in his famous "Astrology Reexamined:"

In analyzing a birth chart I recognized that the distribution of 3 planets by zodiac sign would be $(12)^3$ or 1728 possible combinations, 4 planets by sign 20,000 possible combinations, all the planets plus the Sun and Moon would be $(12)^{10}$ or 60 billion possible combinations by sign alone. Every possible combination in a birth chart of signs, points, planets, houses and aspects combined becomes 10^{35}; by contrast an estimate of the number of grains of sand on all the beaches of the world is 10^{27}.

Dr. Chen had found a model for his holistic operating system. If his assumptions were correct, an android operating system based upon this holistic model could accomplish two things:

1) **Simulate human consciousness, responding naturally and creatively to momentary possibilities.**
2) **Be programed to match the astrological paradigm of their primary human assignment.**

Zhou Xingjia knew this story well. Dr. Chen Wu Chen's assumptions had been proved correct. His landmark research and mathematical algorithms had finally won him a Nobel Prize in Science in 2113, and as Director of BHAI's android development he continued to oversee what had become a trillion RMB (Chinese currency "Renminbi") global enterprise. Nothing the Americans or Europeans had could match what BAI did, nor keep-up with what BHAI had done since and was still doing

9

Still gazing out the window 70-stories up, Xingjia wondered how this day would play-out in her story as well. She could barely stand the suspense. Every doubt played upon her mind. She was thirty-two now, successful by every professional measure. Yet personal relationships had not led to marriage, only "learning experiences" as she framed it. Now she was poised for a new learning experience, her own companion. Any minute the glass doors behind her would slide open, and she would meet "him." "It would be the first of something…" she thought, and then trembled slightly as she heard the glass doors open. Closing her eyes for a second, she inhaled, opened her eyes and turned to meet him.

CHAPTER TWO

HIM

Two handsome men who appeared to be in their early thirties and an attractive slightly older, woman wearing glasses, walked towards Xingjia. Taken aback, Xingjia tried to hide her puzzlement.

"Hi, I'm Dr. Wang," the woman greeted – extending her hand. Smiling graciously to hide her amusement at Xingjia's confusion, she began to make introductions.

"This is Dr. Li." Xingjia shook his hand, as her now knowing but disbelieving eyes turned away from Dr. Li to face the other man.

"And I'm *not* a doctor," the other man said, smiling slightly, "at least not yet." Xingjia, dropped her hand from the handshake with the doctor. Her knees were trembling slightly. Her mind saying, *this is him... this is him...*

He was slightly tall, well proportioned, somewhat athletic looking, handsome – *yes,* she thought. He had a somewhat angular jade shaped face, but something in his eyes was unexpected, sympathetic, attentive and impossibly *familiar.*

"... my name is Huang Bei," he said, breaking the awkward silence.

"Huang... Bei?" Xingjia repeated, puzzled by his given name.

"Bei, yes, I know it's different, but I chose it because it means 'north.' Like the needle on a compass, you know, providing direction..."

Dr. Wang and Dr. Li both seemed amused - chuckling as Xingjia extended her hand saying,

"I'm Xingjia, Zhou Xingjia." After which she quickly added, "providing direction for whom?" She noticed his hand was warm and firm.

"What? Oh? I don't know? I wasn't thinking of it like that. There's just something reassuring about a compass."

"Unless you're close to magnetic north," Xingjia countered, wondering why she was saying this even as she said it, "then the compass needle just spins round and round aimlessly."

Huang Bei laughed, it was a warm laugh, a good laugh. Xingjia hated how much she liked his laugh.

Dr. Wang intervened, "Xingjia, Dr. Li and I are going to leave you and Bei alone, now... so you can begin to get to know each other better. You know, we are looking forward to reading your relationship journal. From both of you."

"Both of us, right..." Xingjia repeated, seeming slightly distracted, as she tried not to look at Bei.

"Yes, remember? All couples are asked to provide a relationship journal. You don't have to divulge anything you're not comfortable with; we respect your privacy of course."

"Yes," Xingjia replied, "yes, of course, I know."

"We understand that this is a new experience for you, for both of you... It's okay to feel nervous at first," Dr. Wang reassured.

"Think of it as a first date," Dr. Li added.

"Or, whatever?" Dr. Wang countered, glancing at Dr. Li disapprovingly. "Of course, you'll need to contact our counseling services within 3-days; you're automatically registered. I know you're familiar with the protocol."

"Yes, yes, of course," Xingjia replied, "I helped write some of the upgrades."

"Xingjia works in our humanistic counseling development department," Dr. Wang reminded Dr. Li. "Okay, well, we'll leave you two alone now."

"Goodbye, Bei" Dr. Wang said warmly.

"I'll beat you next time," Dr. Li said to Bei, pointing at him as he left.

Xingjia and Bei watched them walk away. "Beat you at what?" Xingjia asked.

"Ping pong," Bei replied.

"Oh," Xingjia remarked, unable to hide her nervousness.

"Listen, we can do whatever you like?" Bei said reassuringly. "We don't have to hang around here. There's a park less than three blocks away, out of the south entrance."

"Okay, sure, why not," Xingjia replied.

On the crowded elevator on the way down, Xingjia noticed a group of teenage girls that were part of a tour of BHAI. They were eyeing Bei, and giggling. Bei turned around and smiled at them. They giggled more. Xingjia shook her head disbelievingly. "Were you flirting with those girls?" she asked, as they got off the elevator.

"Look at me," Bei said. Xingjia stopped and looked questioningly at him. "Look at my neck," he asked, "do you see a bolt sticking out of my neck?"

"What?" She asked.

"Do you see a bolt sticking out of my neck?" he asked again.

"No," she replied, trying to grasp his meaning.

"Good. I thought maybe that's what they were laughing at." Bei said, suddenly grinning, and walking away towards the exit, laughing.

Xingjia was stunned. *This guy, this – whatever he was – had a sense of humor. He had a sense of humor!* She just stood there, smiling, momentarily confused, watching him walk towards the exit for a few more seconds.

He held the door for her politely, waiting, looking knowingly bemused as she walked by him and stepped outside.

13

Huang Bei was technically only 78 days old on February 27, 2121, the day that he and Xingjia met, and went for a stroll in the park. Though his many android and AI features were manufactured and installed at earlier dates and times, he was awakened on December 11, 2120 at 10:25 PM in Kunshan, China. The date and time of his awakening was chosen for astrological reasons. Though his astro-algorithmic patterning was designed to match Xingjia's AstroPsychology companion profile, researchers had discovered that companions performed in a measurably more enhanced manner when awakened at a specific date and time that also resonated astrologically with their human assignment. Dr. Chen Wu Chen had explained it this way in a recent article: "AstroPsychology can be divided into categories of resonance. Each category contains a variable of potentiality that can be matched with others who share the same category. The similarities make for familiarity and rapport, while the variables facilitate uniqueness." Dr. Chen's theory applied to both animate and inanimate objects, which had made him unpopular with some scientists and many religious leaders. "Ancient people didn't make this distinction," Dr. Chen would say, citing the anthropological/historical record of native peoples worldwide, such as native American tribes that saw both a rock, a tree, and a person, as equally alive in their own way, possessing a spirit or "vibration," as Dr. Chen was fond of saying, "a vibration that can be expressed mathematically in algorithms. Algorithms that provide proofs and demonstrate the connectedness of our universe."

"Connectedness is the creative network of compatibility," Dr. Chen was fond of saying, in reference to his enhanced companion creation. "We exploit this connectedness by relying upon patterns that are essentially cosmic in nature, what we call AstroPsychological." What this meant in terms of Zhou Xingjia, was that her birthdate of December 10, 2088 at 11:48 AM in Beijing, China had an astrological structure that could be represented as a unique mathematical algorithm. The pattern of this algorithm operated like a fractal in the creation of each unique synthetic neural network of a companion. The result was that every companion matched their assigned person in ways that felt incredibly familiar to the person. However, as Dr. Chen and his staff at BHAI had discovered, the result of such familiar resonance frequently had the side effect of amplifying unresolved issues in the person. Counseling protocols had to be established early on to deal with these side effects, which could not always be easily resolved. In extreme cases, a companion had to be permanently disassociated from their assigned person, though such cases were rare – numbering only 1/1000. In most cases, the person's LFR, or Life Fulfillment Ratio, improved significantly, though ninety-three percent required counseling, and fifty-seven percent of these for an average of two-years. Counseling was accepted as a necessary component of achieving a successful LFR, something that Xingjia knew as well as anyone, since she worked in the Holistic Counseling Development Department of BHAI.

However, as Zhou Xingjia was now realizing as she strolled through the park with Huang Bei, on an unusually warm late February day, no amount of academic study, protocol development, or counseling practice could fully prepare someone for what it was like to be in the presence of their own companion. To passers-by she and Bei were just another couple, taking advantage of a beautiful day to walk together in the park. It was hard for Xingjia not to feel this way too, but she knew better and knowing the truth made her guarded and uneasy. She knew objectively this was a common reaction at first, but she hadn't expected how intense her feelings would be. "Maybe I'm overreacting," she said to herself, but she knew she was rationalizing. She knew she had to acknowledge her feelings without judgment, like she herself had told many others in her work.

15

"You know, these Gingko's are unique," Bei said, interrupting her silent introspection, as his hand patted the trunk of a large tree still bare of leaves.

"What?" Xingjia replied, "how so?" She couldn't imagine why he was talking about trees.

"Their DNA exactly matches the same strand of Gingko's that grow next to the original Shou Lin Temple in Henan."

"Okay?" Xingjia said, wondering where this was going...

"It suggests, that monks from Shou Lin planted their Gingko ancestors here, perhaps some 1,500 years ago."

"How do you know all this?" Xingjia asked.

"Botany is one of my specialties. Plants share the world, co-created the world, the biosphere people take for granted. Photosynthesis is their gift, their way of giving back." Bei paused, pensive.

"Listen..." he said.

Xingjia looked at him, his eyes were thoughtful, even sympathetic.

"We have options, you know?" he said.

"Options? What do you mean?" Xingjia asked.

"I could get a job. I could work. I'm quite capable of earning a living. After all, it's a big chunk of your pay check that's paying for this relationship."

Xingjia was not prepared for this conversation. In fact, she didn't feel prepared for anything at the moment. She could only think of an obvious question.

"Where would you live?" She blurted out, not fully realizing all that her question implied.

"Oh, there are dormitories for the likes of me." Bei replied, nonchalant.

"Yes, I suppose there are." Xingjia said.

"It would give us time to get to know each other, without any pressure." Bei paused, adding "A percentage of my income would also reduce the amount of your installments."

Bei smiled slightly.

Xingjia looked daringly at him. "What if I wanted to take you home with me now and explore your other options?"

"I wouldn't object." Bei replied, without a hint of sarcasm, but then, looking curious he asked, "Is that what you'd like to do?"

Xingjia had felt her pulse rising the second of her daring innuendo. Now she was savoring the excitement and fighting her urge to take full advantage of this handsome... guy. Yet, part of her wanted to break into a run and jog all 7 kilometers' home.

"I like options," was all she could answer.

"Yes, so do I," Bei countered, leaning against the Ginkgo. "But couples that become intimate too soon, tend to face more..."

"Interpersonal challenges." Xingjia interrupted, finishing his statement. "Yes, I know. I'm familiar with the protocol."

"Of course, you are," Bei said, knowingly.

"Oh, so what else do you already know about me?" Xingjia countered, still feeling impulsive.

"It's not like that," Bei replied.

"Like what?" Xingjia asked.

"It's not *programming.* I was just curious, so I asked about you." Bei stated, actually looking a bit defensive. "I wanted to know more about you."

"So, what did you find out?" Xingjia said teasingly, moving closer to him.

"I know your birth date, and your favorite color, *teal*, and that you scored in the upper 5% scholastically of your AstroPsychology class."

"So, you think you know me?" Xingjia asked, looking him in the eyes. Those incredible eyes.

"Not yet," Bei answered, locking eyes with her.

All she could think was, "could he ever know me? How could he *ever _ know _ me?* And what would his knowingness mean? The illusion of compatibility?!" Suddenly Xingjia was seized with regret. This was a mistake. Despite all her efforts to have no preconceived expectations, all she could feel was sad. Terribly, embarrassingly sad.

"Let's walk some more," Bei suggested.

"Sure," Xingjia shrugged.

They walked silently towards a pond, where white ducks who had thus far survived the winter paddled about beyond the melting ice that still clung to the reeds near the shore.

The wind had begun to gust around the buildings that evening, as Xingjia pushed her way through the revolving doors of her favorite restaurant. She looked around for her friend Mei, who waved her over to a small table. Mei was tall and slim, taller than Xingjia. She had knowing eyes and a wicked sense of humor, *dangerous for sensitive types and weakened egos*, Xingjia remembered her saying, but Xingjia loved Mei's honesty – even when she didn't agree with her. And tonight, she needed Mei, and she needed that frothy purple drink in the brandy snifter that Mei had waiting for her. She took a big sip.

"So, where is he?" Mei asked.

"Checked into his dormitory," Xingjia said, wiping the purple froth from her upper lip.

"That's boring," Mei said, frowning. "I thought you'd at least tell me he was home cooking a gourmet dinner, and making sure his amorous assessments were in good working order for you later."

"I sent you a photo," Xingjia said, continuing to frown.

"I got it. He's gorgeous, darling," Mei said, eyeing her friends face, "So why so gloomy? He looks like a stud to me."

"He's not a gigolo, you know." Xingjia snapped.

"Yes, well he'd be a ridiculously expensive prostitute if he were," Mei countered. "So, what is it? Didn't you two hit it off?"

"Maybe... I don't know; he's very real you know. More real than I imagined he would be. I mean, I've seen lots of companions before at work. They're always polite, intelligent, and *normal*, but they... seem preoccupied... like they're focused on something else."

"You mean on *someone* else, don't you?" Mei said. "All the companions I've ever talked to seemed like dogs that belonged to someone else. You could pet them, but their attention was always on their owner."

"That's horrible, Mei!"

"We'll," Mei shrugged, "it's true, isn't it?"

"No, it's *not* true. They're not dogs. They're not pets. They're capable of interacting on an extremely high level, not only in terms of IQ but EQ!"

"So, you liked him. I get it. You're so supposed to be compatible, right? But that's the problem, isn't it? You like him, but you know he's not real. So, you feel like you're being deceived, and this pisses you off."

"Maybe," Xingjia replied, toying with her nearly empty glass.

"Maybe exactly," Mei pronounced knowingly, "you want another drink?"

While Mei flagged the waiter down, Xingjia could only think "What is real? What do we mean by real? He's real enough, isn't he? He looked at me like no one has ever looked at me. How is that possible? Am I just projecting, imagining that he experiences me? I wonder what he does experience?" Xingjia wished that her second drink would come soon.

For ten years, ever since companions had fully emerged on the scene, debates had raged worldwide like a philosophical inferno. On the spiritual or religious side, the outcry was "they have no souls." Those who believed in reincarnation were left to speculate how companions fit into the many lives scheme of things. Some wondered whether or not *inception*, the term for a soul's entry into the body, might occur when companions were *awakened*, but most rejected such an idea as outrageous and assumed reincarnation would continue the way it always had. Superstitious types saw companions as soulless automatons to be feared rather than welcomed into society. Those who mistrusted science, were quick to point out that science could not always accurately predict outcomes, fueling the usual horror scenarios of a future where companions took over the world and eliminated humans. There had even been some acts of violence towards companions in the west, where groups had organized in protest, claiming that companions disrupted the "natural order," offending God and nature. Some environmentalists had joined with those on the religious right in the U.S. to denounce companions, organizing legal action to prevent their further development and integration into society.

The scientific community had no such philosophical or religious qualms. Sociologists gathered data and analyzed results, presenting their findings regarding the introduction of companions in society. Socioeconomic statistics revealed the economic reality, and the impact upon the work force. That China, the most populous nation in the world, a nation with the largest work force, would lead the world in the production of androids and companions, seemed incredibly ironic. Why would a nation with so many people to employ need androids? As it turned out, China's economic expansion, which had long surpassed the U.S., now dominated the world. Such global economic domination was in fact the result of the manufacture and export of robotics, androids, and now companions. BHAI was only the latest development company to emerge from a mega-industry that employed hundreds of millions in China. The growing popularity of companions may have stirred deep controversy and debate in many parts of the world, but in China, companions were seen as simply the latest fascinating line in an evolution of robotics and android products. Robotics and androids had brought about the economic miracle China had been searching for a hundred years previously.   Companions were to be applauded, not feared.

To most scientists, a companion was simply a highly-sophisticated *device*. As such, it was considered as property, and regulated according to each countries legal definition of property. In China, when someone purchased a companion, which was an expense comparable to the cost of a small apartment, they were actually *leasing* the companion only for the length of *their* life. The lease was non-transferable, and no companion could legally be sold. At the time of their death, custody of a companion would revert to BHAI, and the disassociated companion would be recycled following a period of debriefing, within which the complex memory of the companion would be logged-in and chronicled. More than simply a journal, the memory of a companion contained a unique multi-faceted individual history. Already, Dr. Chen Wu Chen and his team of researchers were intrigued by this record of a companion's history, which they believed would prove incredibly valuable in understanding companions, and of course, suggest new ways to improve design and functionality.

However, companions had only been on the market for 10-years; with 54% of customers being young professional women in their thirties. So, the number of companions available for debriefing had been limited. Nonetheless, information obtained from debriefing had already influenced the most recent round of companion development, including Huang Bei. In fact, the customers who acquired these most recent companion models, had been carefully selected. Unbeknownst to Zhou Xingjia, she belonged to a select international customer base, a base that had its own file and special project label at BHAI. Her journal entries would be carefully monitored, along with Huang Bei's. Dr. Chen himself was deeply curious regarding the latest companion-couple journal input, and surprised his team by becoming directly involved in reading and analyzing journal entries. Nothing yet seemed different than with previous companion couples. Yet, Dr. Chen remained attentive, often working later than had been his habit for some time. Whatever his interest or concerns were, he had not divulged them to anyone.

Yet, on this night, while Xingjia sipped drinks with Mei, and Huang Bei adjusted to life in his new dormitory, Dr. Chen was looking at the birth chart of Xingjia and the *awakening* chart of Bei. Despite all the sophisticated data at his disposal, Dr. Chen liked studying these old astrological charts. Sipping his "hong cha," Dr. Chen considered the current trends for Xingjia and Bei, contemplating what this might mean for them, and simultaneously wondering where all of this might lead. He could not be sure of how things would go from here. The outcome so far over the last ten years had exceeded his expectations. Yet, Dr. Chen could not shake a vague uneasiness mixed with wonder within himself, something that no equation could satisfy, as he stared out over the nightscape of glittering Beijing.

CHAPTER THREE

ADJUSTMENTS

Only hours before, Huang Bei had followed the resident associate or "RA" down the hall of his new dormitory. Noticing an occasional open door, he had estimated how much smaller the rooms were than at the Orientation Center – where he had 12 square meters to himself. He estimated 10 square meters now, with a roommate.

"You're getting a room at the end," the RA had told him, "they have two windows instead of one and the best view."

Bei considered this information. Two windows instead of one. He wondered if there was a reason for this. Was it random? Or had he been assigned a room with two windows for some purpose. He had compiled a list of explanations, prioritizing within a second the most plausible to the least. At the top of the list was, 1) *Sun in Sagittarius in H4, if in a small room one needs at least a good view to avoid feeling trapped.* He made a mental note with amusement, "It was chosen for me." He saved his note. He was reasonably sure that Dr. Wang and Dr. Li had selected the room for him, perhaps even Dr. Chen had a say in it. Bei remembered his time with Dr. Chen well. Dr. Chen had personally conducted some of the final testing of Bei's high level functionality. It had been a satisfying experience for Bei.

In their short time together, Bei had identified Dr. Chen as a kind of father figure. "You know, you're the closest thing I'll ever have to a father," Bei had told Dr. Chen at the completion of the last test. Dr. Chen had at first looked caught off-guard but then he appeared thoughtful.

"Only a few have said this," Dr. Chen remarked, "a few of your brothers and sisters – you might say."

"I have siblings?" Bei had questioned, unable to grasp at first what Dr. Chen meant.

"Well, let's say you belong to a unique family. Three other companions that belong to your new group have said something similar. This is a new development, and I'm… rather, "we" are hoping to learn what it means."

Bei did not know what this meant either, but he had made a note about having *siblings*. It was not information he would ever delete. Since then he had reviewed Dr. Chen's curious statement about "a new development" several times. It was like a puzzle, and Bei liked puzzles. Yet this was a puzzle without enough information for Bei.

When they arrived at his dorm room the door had been closed. Bei affirmed his information, Building 1, room 618, as the RA had pressed a button beside the door that emitted what sounded like acoustic guitar cords. "He might be shut-down. No need to trigger a start," the RA had explained, opening the door. It was dark inside. "Li Jian…" the RA had called out. "Why?" said a voice out of the darkness, "Why?"

Bei could see the puzzled look on the RA's face, as the RA had reached inside to turn on the light.

"I don't require a light," Li Jian stated firmly. Li Jian was seated on his bed on the opposite side of the room, holding a wafer-thin phone. "I can see perfectly well in the dark," he said.

"Yes, well… your new roommate is here," the RA explained.

"Fine," Li Jian replied, as he continued to be preoccupied with his phone, ignoring them.

"He only arrived yesterday," the RA had whispered to Bei.

"I can hear you," Li Jian said, without looking up.

"Well, good. Okay then. If you have any questions, there's a screen beside your bed, and all the tools you might need are in the drawer," the RA had gestured towards a desk. "There's a cleaning room down the hall, about 5 doors down."

"Yes, we passed it just now. Thank you," Bei had said politely, extending his hand to the RA.

Bei had noticed the RA's look of surprise at his offer of a handshake and his brief hesitation before shaking hands. Closing the door behind the RA, Bei had casually eyed Li Jian then looked out the window. He considered the trees in the courtyard below; they had passed them on the way in. He could see the dark windows and a smattering of lights in the buildings across the way. It was quiet. Bei thought about Xingjia. She had said she was meeting a friend tonight. "Mei," he recalled. He noticed his energy level was at 52%. He turned the light out. Retrieving a cord from his bag he plugged-in next to his bed. Unbuttoning his shirt, he had connected the other end of the cord to his PPI (personal plug-in) just inside of his navel. He liked the slight buzz of renewing his energy. He had tried to explain this to Dr. Wang. She had compared it to the "goose-bumps" that people get. He didn't know. In the darkness, he could see the light of his roommate's phone. He closed his eyes, his buzz was on. In an hour, he would shut down.

Xingjia was on her third drink, when Mei brought two guys over to the table with her. One was Chinese and the other European, blond – he looked Scandinavian. "Meet Zhang Wei and Neal... what was it?" Mei asked. "Karlsson," he replied, "Just call me Neal," he said in English."

"Oh, you're American?" Xingjia said, "I thought maybe you were Swedish."

"Swedish ancestors," he replied. "Your English is excellent, by the way."

"Thank you," Xingjia, said smiling at him. She leaned close to Mei, whispering "I thought you said you were just going to the bathroom?"

"I couldn't resist," Mei replied, under her breath – smiling at the guys.

"We're here for a conference. This place was recommended to us by a Beijing guy," Wei said. "I'm from Xi'an." He took a quick sip, "We're in software development."

"For pilot-droids," Neal added.

"Oh, I just love those pilot voices," Mei says, imitating them, "welcome, to China's Premier Airline, Air China. Relax in comfort, and discover that flying near the speed of sound is quiet, peaceful, and luxurious. You'll arrive before you know it, wishing you could stay onboard."

Everyone laughed. Xingjia noticed Mei cuddling-up to Wei. She exchanged glances with Neal. He's handsome. He seems like a nice guy. *Probably married*, she thought.

"This is my first visit to China," Neal announced.

"Oh, a virgin!" Mei said. Wei laughed. Neal looked sheepish.

"Well, don't worry honey," Mei said, "We'll take good care of you. Won't we, darling?" Mei added, nodding at Xingjia. Xingjia did not answer. She looked at Neal blankly, and then smiled.

"I need some time alone with Neal," Xingjia suddenly announced, grabbing Neal's hand she led him past the bar towards the hallway that led to the bathrooms.

Neal looked confused.

"Kiss me," she said.

Neal complied. "Oh shit," Xingjia thought, "he's a good kisser." She broke away from their kiss.

"I know you're married," Mei said, looking straight into his green eyes.

"Okay," Neal confessed. "I'm married, and you're gorgeous. Two honest statements."

"So, betraying your wife is honest?" She asked, looking frankly at him.

"I don't know how to answer that," he replied.

"You don't have to answer it, at least – not because of me. You're sweet." She patted his hand, then led him back to the table.

"Where have you two been?" Mei said insinuatingly.

"I've got to go," Xingjia said to Mei.

Mei looked surprised, and then slightly guilty, as she turned to the guys, "I'll be right back."

"Xingjia, I'm sorry. I just wanted us to have some fun, like we used to." Mei said wistfully.

"I know," Xingjia said, making her way towards the door. "I understand, I do."

"So look, what's going to happen if you meet a man you really like – even love? What happens to your relationship with your companion? What happens then?" Mei inquired.

"I'll deal with it when and *if* it happens. That's all I can say right now," Xingjia replied, "okay?"

"Sure, okay. I'm here for you," Mei reassured. "And I want to meet him, okay? Soon!"

Xingjia nodded, and stepped into the night. Once outside, she tried not to think about Mei's question as she looked for her cab. Not thinking about it, meant it was all she would think about on the way home.

Huang Bei had discovered he would often power-on in reaction to the refracted light of dawn. He knew that sunrise was technically at 6:53:54 AM on February 28, 2121 in Beijing, and that he was actually facing South-South-East rather than exactly East, but there he was – awake. Despite an urge to stand-up and look outside, he glanced over at Li Jian. Jian was still focused on his phone, but there was something about his posture and eyes that alerted Bei. Getting-up, Bei came over and felt Jian's wrist. "One percent power," Bei read, digital lights flashing a soft red warning. Bei opened Jian's bedside drawer. Eyeing Jian's E-cord, Bei removed the cord from the drawer. Gently lifting Jian's shirt up to expose his navel, he systematically plugged him in. Jian's eyes registered, fluttering briefly before opening. "Why?" he stuttered softly. Bei looked him over, he seemed perfectly functional.

Bei thought about going down the hall to the cleaning room.

Suddenly Jian looked at him, offering Bei his phone screen to look at. "Li Na," he said. "This is Li Na."

Bei looked at Jian's phone. The clear image of a woman in her late thirties looked back at him. The angle of the photo made her eyes look too large, but Bei could see that her face conformed to 88.4% perfect symmetry – a classic beauty. "Nice," Bei responded, politely.

"Nice?" Jian replied, voice raised in a mock question. "Nice..." his voice trailed. Sitting up straighter he said, "Maybe that's what I'll say when they debrief me. She was *nice*." Jian looked at Bei. "My texts are blocked, my calls. It's over. I'm over. It's the only conclusion I can come to. I tried to reach her 3,601 times in the last 10-hours. I only hope she's okay. The man she's with has a Moon-Mars conjunction in Aries, within 1.4-degrees. I detected adrenal stress in his interactions with Li Na, 27-times in the last month. She ignored my findings."

"Your, findings? You mean, you told her this?" Bei questioned. "You warned her that he had a quick temper, and an average of 19.6 % potential to react physically when angry?"

"I printed it out and pasted it on our bathroom mirror," Jian said matter of factly, "After posting it in my journal, of course."

"How long have you two been together?" Bei asked.

"First time, twenty-two months, 27 days, and 9.45 hours. Then, a 3-month 3 day and 7.2-hour break. Then we were companions again for twenty-two months, 28 days, and 21.3 hours. Now, it's been less than 2-days, by 6.7 hours."

"Okay... well, I'm sure you've noticed the pattern." Bei stated calmly.

"Pattern? Sure." Jian, looked up, "What pattern?"

"It's a Mars cycle." Bei answered. "Suggesting, that you'll likely to be with her again in 89 days, 16.2 hours, or so."

"Unless, she decides to pay the *fee*." Jian said.

"You mean, the disassociation fee?" Bei asked.

"Of course, what else?" Jian said.

"What kind of transits is she having?" Bei asked.

"Uranus opposite the Sun," Jian said, "before that, it was Uranus conjunct Mars."

"Well, she's experimenting," Bei said. "Obviously, she was born with a Sun-Mars opposition and Mars in Cancer, so, that's why she likes the Aries-Moon-Mars theme in this new guy. Isn't that part of your profile?"

"Of course!" Jian replied. "If I could, I would've broken his leg. She'd have no respect for a guy that's an invalid."

"Yes, well, thank Dr. Chen for that protocol."

"Who?" Jian said, picking his phone up again and starring at Li Na's photo.

Bei decided not to answer. This conversation had lost its buzz for Bei. Besides, his readings reminded him it might be a good time to visit the cleaning room. He checked his phone; no messages. An image of Xingjia appeared next to her I.D. He clicked on her image. "Yes, 82.7% perfect symmetry," he said to himself. *Her* eyes *were* a bit large, Pisces Rising, and slightly askew, Uranus conjunct the ASCN. There was a subtle daringness in her face as well, a hint of risk and the unexpected. "Uniquely attractive," Bei thought, "more interesting…" "Of course, I *would* think that." He said to himself, quickly clicking his phone blank and leaving Jian alone still staring at Li Na's photo.

Proficiency in landscape design, along with his expertise in botany, had enabled Bei to easily line-up a job. Two weeks previously, while still living at the Orientation Center, Bei had submitted his CV to China's largest architectural firm R. Lu, originally out of Hong Kong a century ago but now headquartered in Beijing. Dr. Wang and Dr. Chen had been impressed by Bei's initiative and confidence, though Bei offered logical reasons for his actions. "Xingjia will want a more independent companion, someone that can be successful on their own... and, as a Sagittarius my independence and freedom is important to me too, is it not?"

Dr. Wang, had added, "Yes, but you're more domestic and family oriented than she is. So, you'll tend to counterbalance her emphasis on career."

Bei had smiled at Dr. Wang and Dr. Chen, "So, does this mean I'm expected do the dishes?"

Dr. Wang and Dr. Chen were delighted by Bei's confident self-assessment and his dry sense of humor. Bei sometimes expressed his observations with a twist of humor only seen in the most recent Huang series of companions.

So it was, that Huang Bei rode the subway to his new job at R. Lu, on Wednesday morning, February 28, 2121, looking no different than any other *handsome* professional man in his thirties on the way to work. Of course, his supervisor and co-workers were well-aware of Bei's identity. He was the first companion to ever work in their landscape design department, so everyone was curious – some even apprehensive. However, by lunchtime, the impression shared by all was how "normal" he seemed. "You know, that's the scary thing," one woman confessed to a female colleague at lunch, "you can't really tell that he's *not* human?"

"I know," her friend agreed, "but I'll bet there's a way we could find out?" They both giggled.

However, not needing to eat, Bei had decided to use his lunch hour to visit the cactus garden on the 17th floor. He was closely examining the waxy bright yellow blossoms of a North American prickly pear cactus when he saw a call coming in from Xingjia.

"Hello..."

"Hi," Xingjia said, sounding hesitant at first. "So, did you get moved in last night?"

"Yes."

"Okay." Xingjia viewed a locator map on her phone. "So, what are you doing in an office building at the corner of Ritanbei Lu and Gongtidong Lu?"

"Actually, I'm in the cactus garden on the 17th floor, on my lunch break."

Silence.

"Cactus garden?" Silence. "Lunch break? You're having *lunch*?"

"Yes, yes and then no. Let me explain. I started a job today, and I'm on my lunch break."

"A job!? You already have a job!?"

"Yes. You didn't object to this yesterday when I told you I could get a job and contribute financially. Did I misread you?"

"No, but you didn't tell me you already *had* a job. Or, did you just go out and get one *today*?"

"I was interviewed two weeks ago. Today was my first day."

"Well, you could've told me!?" Xingjia sounded totally perplexed.

"The job's been on hold. It just seemed like the right thing to do." Bei said matter-of-factly. "I hadn't heard anything from you, so when they called me and asked me if I could start today, I said 'yes."

"Well, aren't you Mr. Independent," Xingjia said. "Do you have any other plans I should know about?"

Bei paused. "No, but I was wondering what you're doing for dinner tonight?"

Silence.

"I don't know."

"What about some home cooking?" Bei asked, walking over to the double paned large glass window.

"You're inviting me to come over and have dinner at *your place*?" Xingjia said, confused.

"I don't have a kitchen." Bei replied.

Silence.

31

"Okay, so you're inviting me to *my* kitchen for a home cooked meal – is, that right?"

"Yes."

"That's a first," she said.

"For me too." Bei replied.

Xingjia laughed, amused and incredulous at the same time.

"You're too much," She said finally.

"So, what would you like? What's your favorite cuisine?" Bei asked.

"You don't know? I thought you already knew everything about me?"

"I'm learning," Bei replied.

Xingjia laughed, and said "Surprise me. I like surprises."

"Okay," Bei said, "What time should I arrive?"

"Make it 6:30. That should work."

"Okay, I'll be at your door with the groceries."

Xingjia teased him. "Some delivery guy."

Bei smiled. "Well, at least this way, if you change your mind you can keep the groceries."

Xingjia laughed. "I gotta go, okay? I'll see you tonight."

Xingjia sat at her desk, her amusement fading. "He's coming over tonight. He's coming over *tonight!* Maybe it's not such a good idea. Maybe I should call him back and cancel." She felt immobilized. Finally, it occurred to her, "Maybe I should check out the transits for tonight…"

Bei stared thoughtfully out the window at the cars and people below. He would have just enough time to shop for groceries after 5:00 and arrive at 6:30.

Xingjia looked at herself in the mirror. She heard an old familiar superficial judgment in her head, temporarily reclaiming its opinion of her. *I'm funny looking. I am. I look strange, no matter what I do. I thought my strangeness would wear-off a little as I got older, but no – I look stranger all the time.* She began to brush her hair in a different direction. She remembered that when she was a teenager she used to believe there was another *her* – an ideal her, a her with 100% perfect facial symmetry with no freckles, living an ideal life in another dimension. As a serious student of AstroPsychology, she had grown to understand that as someone with Pisces Rising, she could easily imagine an ideal self, even an ideal appearance. And, what can compare to an ideal? An ideal is like a statue of Quan Lin or Mother Mary, we glimpse her in others in part, but never fully. She had struggled to realize, that even though an ideal can inspire, in comparison it provides a place to hide. She didn't want to hide anymore. She felt ready to live her life more fully than ever, to accept her Uranian strangeness. *I'm a mutant,* she laughed to herself. *And, why should it matter anyway? This... guy, was made to like me! He's going to like me no matter what. He's going to like me regardless of how smart I am, regardless of what I wear, or my hair, or make-up or anything, right? So, why do I want to impress him? Is it just a habit? A guy's coming over, and I have to impress him?* She stared at herself, as she began to understand. *If he accepts me no matter what, then I come face-to-face with any part of myself that I haven't accepted.*

She sighed, *this is all too much for a dinner date, especially in my own kitchen.* She teasingly thought, *I should've slept with Mr. Blonde last night, then maybe I would've said 'no' today.* She knew she was just searching for a way to put-off what felt so inevitable. *But only change and death are inevitable,"* she said to herself, closing her eyes. *Calm down. Relax. You know yourself well. Everything is going to be fine. Life is an adventure. It will take you where you need to go.*

A sudden knock at the door startled her and she yelped!

CHAPTER FOUR

HOME COOKING

S he pulled her dress down more snuggly, as she approached the door. Her dress was an old favorite, very soft and familiar against her skin. She opened the door.

Suddenly she didn't know what to say.

Bei stood there, looking at her questioningly? "Your groceries, Mam." So, should I just leave them here?"

"Oh! Sorry! Come in, come in! "Follow me. The kitchen is right over here."

Bei set the two bags on the kitchen counter.

"So, what are we having tonight?" She asked, posing teasingly. "God, am I posing?" she said to herself, and changed her posture.

"Italian," Bei said.

"Really?"

"Well, I know you have the Moon in the 9th House and Sun in Sagittarius, and that you went to Italy when you were twenty-four. So, I guessed you might like foreign cuisine... Was I wrong?" Italy! Bei could not have been more-right. Xingjia had spent one incredible month in Italy back in July of 2113, when transiting Jupiter was stationary in Scorpio on her Moon. She loved the food, had a passionate affair with a beautiful man named Stephano, and had even entertained the idea of moving there. Stephano had only texted her for two weeks after she returned to China, yet despite her disappointment, she had saved the photos of the two of them from that romantic summer. She cherished her passionate memories and remained addicted to Italian cuisine.

"I love Italian food. It's... so sensuous." She said, feeling that her words were inadequate. She enjoyed watching Bei busily moving about her kitchen. Her cooking utensils, and pots and pans hung from the wall, making it easy to find things.

Water heated in a big pot, while he chopped basil, garlic, and then tomatoes on the cutting board next to her big skillet. The aromas of basil and garlic were almost intoxicating.

"Tomatoes are not native to Italy, you know?" Bei commented.

"Oh?"

"They came to Italy from South America, over fifty years after Columbus." He said, cutting a slice of juicy red tomato and offering it to her to taste.

As she took the slice into her mouth some of the tomato juice squirted from her lips and down her chin. She laughed at herself...

Bei offered her a napkin. "In colonial America, tomatoes were called 'love apples."

"Love apples?" she asked.

"Yes, though some thought they were poisonous, others believed their red color meant they would excite passion in those that ate them."

Xingjia watched as he poured olive oil into a small glass bowl and scraped some of the minced garlic and basil into the bowl. Cutting off a small corner of bread, he dipped it into the olive oil and offered her a taste. She closed her eyes as she tasted the fresh bread soaked in olive oil with garlic and basil.

As she savored this sumptuous morsel, it occurred to her, "he's not tasting anything. I wonder if he *can* taste?" She thought. For a second she hesitated. "Do you mind if I ask you something?" she said.

"Sure, ask me anything," he replied, smoothly opening a bottle of Chianti.

"Can... you taste things?"

Bei grinned slightly, "what kind of chef would I be if I couldn't taste things?"

"So, that's a yes?" She asked.

"Yes." He answered, as he began to pour a little wine into *two* glasses.

"Can you taste this?" she said, turning him towards her, and gently bringing his lips to hers.

Bei spilled red wine on the counter as they kissed, though he managed to set the bottle down. Xingjia knew good kissers, and though shy at first – Bei's response was everything she liked. Bei himself, was inundated with tastes, the bread, the garlic, the basil, the olive oil, and especially Xingjia's pheromones flooding his sensory receptors in an overwhelming chemical mix...

Xingjia pulled away from their kiss, and took him by the hand coaxing him away from the kitchen. He reached back and cut off the stove. She led him quietly towards her bedroom. The spilled red wine would remain on the counter for now.

Bei lay quietly next to Xingjia while she slept. He listened to the rhythm of her breathing. Her breaths came easily, a soft pleasant rhythmic sound Bei thought. His mind absorbed the pattern of her breathing and slowly turned it into music. Her breath formed the underlying rhythm, gentle oboes, clarinets modulating gently, with basset horns, bassoons, more horns and a double base. It was similar to a Mozart serenade for wind-instruments, 3rd movement, *Gran Partitia...* he recalled, listening as the rhythm evolved like a fractal into a landscape of trees and flowers. Bei listened and watched, enthralled for nearly five minutes... until Xingjia unexpectedly spoke a muffled word and turned on her side away from him.

She's dreaming, Bei noted, as he saved the file his mind had just created. He had wondered about dreams. He understood the multi-functional role of dreams, how they regulated the psyche of a person's mind, keeping them sane as their mind free-associated with the representational images of feelings and anxieties unresolved from when they were awake. Bei had theorized that the creativity of his mind was similar to dreaming, only "I am awake when I dream." Bei had noted.

But tonight, any speculation about dreams was pushed aside by what Bei continued to experience, as he lay there processing his first sex with Xingjia. The images of her face and body randomly replayed in his mind, with startling frequency. Her eyes, the look of pleasure on her face, the movements of her body, streamed in a cascade of imagery...

This was not Bei's first sexual experience. His sexual functionality had been tested at the Orientation Center. It had been a memorable learning process, not only in terms of his own functional development, but in terms of his understanding of human beings. He had seen in Dr. Wang an entirely different side of her personality emerge when she had introduced him to the female staff member called "Lien" who would work physically with him to test his sexual functionality. Dr. Wang had stayed in the room with them, guiding him and showing him what he could do and how to go about it. "I'm going to be your sex coach today," she had announced breezily to him that first morning of the training, but he had noticed a slight flush in her cheeks when she said this and later an increase in her pulse. He had also observed how Dr. Wang had maintained a gentle but firm control over the testing process. Whenever Bei had focused all of his attention on Lien, to make sure he was doing everything correctly, Bei had detected a slight undercurrent of what he identified as jealousy in Dr. Wang. Bei remembered that night, near the end of that week, when Dr. Wang had visited him, "for a little more testing," she had said. Bei had noticed how much more relaxed Dr. Wang had seemed the next day.

However, no matter how fascinating the learning experiences with Dr. Wang and Lien had been, nothing had fully prepared Bei for what sex would be like with Xingjia. Bei understood that he was *made* to like Xingjia, to respond to her face, her voice, her every-thing. In the weeks before he had met Xingjia he had increasingly dwelled upon the reality of his programming bias, but tonight it didn't seem important. Instead, all he wanted to do was listen to her breathing and re-imagine their love making. He felt compelled to look at replays that seemed to highlight her beauty. *Yes, beauty*, he said to himself. *Beauty*, he repeated. *She is like a work of art to me, a living, breathing work-of-art.* He then saw her like a painting on the wall, as he strolled about in a museum finding every picture on the wall to be another painting of Xingjia, each one more beautiful and erotic. Wandering through the museum, as music began to play, Bei was increasingly enraptured, mesmerized by a process he was uncertain he *could* control, his mind in a free-fall of blissful creative imagery and sensation.

Suddenly Xingjia woke up. Her clock said 2:02. Immediately she was aware that she was in bed with Bei. She lay there for a moment, listening. The room was completely silent. She slowly turned and felt Bei with her hand. His skin was smooth and warm. He smelled faintly of cinnamon and *garlic*, "or is that garlic me?" she wondered. Fully awake, she turned to face him. His eyes were closed and he was facing the ceiling. "Bei?" she said, "are you... awake?"

"Yes," he said quietly. "I've been listening to you breathe."

"Is that all," she said lazily.

"Not exactly," he replied.

"I'm starving. Do you think it's too late for us to have dinner?" She asked.

"No... but it may be too late to get the wine stain off your counter."

She giggled, and snuggled-up to him. She kissed his arm.

He smelled faintly of cinnamon and vanilla. *Like something sweet, she thought; God, I'm so hungry!* Her stomach growled.

"I hear your stomach," Bei commented.

"Yes, come on," she said, "let's eat!"

Xingjia's eyes squinted as she turned on the kitchen light, adjusting the brightness down. Bei eyed the countertop. He began to clean up the wine. A light red stain would remain on the countertop. Xingjia came up behind Bei as he arranged things and hugged him. He stopped and turned around. They held each other.

"You'll never get dinner this way," he said.

She kept holding him.

Interrupting the silence, she asked, "so, I guess this was your first time?"

Bei hesitated...

"The first time with you," Bei said.

"Well, I *know* that!" She laughed, looking incredulously at him.

"I underwent functionality testing at the Orientation Center." He said plainly.

"Oh! Right, of course..." she felt foolish to have forgotten this. "Well, you obviously passed their test," she added, giggling with her insinuation...

"I hope I haven't ruined your Pisces Rising fantasy," Bei replied teasingly.

"No, Uranus on my ASC already did that!" She countered.

They both laughed, especially Xingjia.

She stopped laughing and looked into Bei's eyes.

"Actually, I think my fantasy is just beginning," she said.

"Good!" Bei replied.

Soon Xingjia was munching on bread and sipping wine while she watched Bei cook. In no time dinner was ready. It was simple and delicious. Just linguini pasta with basil, tomato, garlic, olive oil and grated parmesan cheese. Xingjia ate voraciously, and drank two glasses of wine.

She noticed that Bei had eaten some of the pasta dish, and sipped some wine. She knew he was simply acting social, making her comfortable while she ate.

For a brief moment, she thought *maybe this is all an act*, but she forced such thoughts out of her mind as she looked at Bei. She wanted to enjoy tonight, regardless... to savor it like the pasta...

He is so good looking, she thought. His arms and shoulders were strong, but not overly developed. He was more physically graceful, like a dancer. Yet, it was something in his eyes and face that drew her in, and relaxed her. Suddenly she knew she wanted to make love again. Nothing else mattered, nothing in the world - just his arms around her. Kissing each other, she breathed in his warmness. He kissed her neck, as she broke away and led him back to the bedroom.

Sunrise came at 6:52:25 AM on Saturday, March 1, 2121. Bei watched Xingjia sleeping in the first light. She looked *peaceful and even more beautiful*, he thought. However, he was distracted and puzzled by his power reading. *It was 2.4% higher than it should've been.* He began running calculations, as he looked around Xingjia's bedroom. He recognized the 2050 retro look, titanium with maroon glass trim, all set against light rose colored walls that suggested an ever-receding field of roses – even the window blinds matched. There were photos of Xingjia on the wall, some with friends and family, and a photo of her parents as newly-weds. Bei was *restless. Side-effects*, he thought. Exactly 64 minutes ago he had implemented a system reboot to disrupt the streaming sounds and images that had followed the second round of love making during the wee hours. He had found the second *after-experience* even more overwhelming than the first, because he *was* overwhelmed – and that was the point. It was as if his mind was not his own exactly, and even now he wasn't sure what *that* meant. All he knew was that he needed to re-organize his mind, to re-establish logical priorities and goals; this was his *knowingness* and he couldn't disregard it – though he also knew he needed to learn how to be more careful.

A reboot in a computer is an easy thing, but Huang Bei was no computer. He was at least 10^{32} times more sophisticated than the common PCS (Personal Computer Systems) that managed everyone's home/apartment, financial accounts, transportation, healthcare and itinerary. A reboot in a companion, unlike the safe "sleep" function that occurred during repowering, had a 9% risk factor of system damage, meaning a companion might seem like someone who has had a stroke in worst cases, or there might be less perceptible damage that could still cause any number of functionality issues. The protocol for a companion reboot made it very clear that reboots should only be done when functional problems could not be diagnosed and automatically corrected. Every reboot increased the probability of system damage, and only a maximum of two reboots a year were recommended. Bei had run a diagnosis 5-times, without any functionality issues being detected – though he had noted a .00435792 surge of memory space use. His main concern was that Xingjia might awaken during his reboot and become unnecessarily alarmed at his unresponsive state. Above all, he did not want to create stress for her. He observed her breathing and eye blinking, and determined that she was deep into her R.E.M. sleep cycle. Only then, had he initiated a total system reboot, a process that had taken 25-minutes.

The first companion models had not come with the ability to initiate a system reboot. Only after five years of production had companions been equipped with a self-initiating capacity to reboot, which had been program-restricted to a total of only 3 times. In each instance a system reboot would automatically result in a message being sent to BHAI's Central Operations, alerting the companion's operational team that a system reboot had occurred. Only the most recent line of companion models had come with an unlimited self-initiating system reboot capacity. However, automatic messages regarding a system reboot were still sent to Central Operations, as part of the ongoing monitoring process that also included extensive analysis of journal entries, and counseling recordings. As it was, once a companion had met their human assignment, they would be prompted by a message every 3-days reminding them it was time to make a journal entry.

The new model series of companions to which Huang Bei belonged had a highly sophisticated self-monitoring system. Dr. Chen had postulated that a companion was now likely to be more self-aware than most humans. Each companion had a complex holistic self-monitoring system, designed up Dr. Chen's original algorithms – permeating every cell of their synthetic neural network. In addition, each companion had the capacity to analyze themselves in astrological terms, based upon the moment of their "awakening." For example, Bei knew he had Neptune in Scorpio in the 3rd house, sextile his Ascendant (ASC), Moon, and Mercury, trine his Saturn and square his Venus. Such a Neptune placement offered Bei a frame of reference that could in part explain the creative imagery that had followed his love making with Xingjia. Bei understood that Scorpio resonated with the experience of passion and Neptune with imagination. Such a 3rd house placement implied a mind readily stimulated by a mix of passion and imagination. Each aspect with Neptune showed the connection with his body (ASC), emotions (Moon), mind (Mercury), and feelings of love and affection (Venus). The square between Neptune in Scorpio and Venus in Aquarius implied a possible conflict between a detached friendly objectivity and overwhelming feelings of undifferentiated love, passion and affection. There was also a close trine between Neptune and Saturn in Bei's awakening-chart, suggesting that Bei could find ways to more easily harmonize the boundlessness of Neptune with Saturn's serious requirement for well-defined boundaries. However, the opposition between Saturn in Cancer and Mercury in Capricorn underlined Bei's need for a more organized mental perspective, as did the down-to-earth logical orientation of his Virgo ASC and Moon. Bei understood this objectively, but he was wrestling with his "experience" – and experience is always more daunting than objectivity.

As it was, Bei could've explained his astrological makeup to you himself, and perhaps he would've done so readily – if anyone had asked him. Dr. Chen had delighted in discussing astrology and Astropsychology with Bei, it had been one of their main topics of conversation. Others had asked Dr. Chen if these companions were really as self-aware as they seemed, or were they just repeating AstroPsychological terms they had been programmed to repeat. For nearly a hundred years Artificial Intelligence had been used in the selling of astrological reports, beginning with very crude limited AI applications as far back as 2018. Over time AI had become incredibly sophisticated at "synthesis," able to create original natural sounding interpretations from any variety of astrological combinations.

However, companions went far beyond such synthesis, measuring their own potential against the framework of their astrological understanding in a variety of unique and creative ways. As Dr. Chen liked to point out, "the self-correcting nature of a companion is enhanced by their astrological frame of reference. We humans could learn from this." Critics thought Dr. Chen had lost his perspective as a scientist, having become overly enamored with his companions, falsely believing them capable of more than was actually possible. Dr. Chen was ridiculed, when he asked, "Why could a companion not know, what we call love?" Yet, he had more to say on the subject. "You say a companion is just a highly-sophisticated device, performing the way they were programmed to behave. Yet, what of we humans? Do we not also behave in ways programmed to a great extent by our biology, a biology we share in one way or another with all life on this planet? And yet we speak of "love" as if it were uniquely human, impossible for other species to understand, much less a tree or a rock." Dr. Chen had been labeled a *mystic* when he then said, "Who knows if a large rock, sitting still and alone for eons, has within itself composed a poem of such depth that could we read it, all would weep with joy."

Dr. Chen would've been fascinated if he could've listened to Huang Bei's continued self-assessment and analysis as he lay next to Xingjia in the morning light. Along with his AstroPsychological musings, Bei also worried that he had rebooted unnecessarily, and had begun to re-examine his reasons for doing so. Suddenly he heard a slight vibration coming from his right. It was his phone. Quietly he reached over to silence the vibration. There were 3 messages, the first was from BHAI CO (Central Operations):

> **2121 March 1 - A class-1 system reboot was reported at 05:49. Please verify that your problem has been resolved by clicking on this icon 👤 and entering your serial number.**

The second message was from Dr. Chen Wu Chen:

> **Bei, Are you alright? Please let me know. You've been in my thoughts. I would like to see you. Just text me when you get a chance. The Moon is in the sign Leo today, perhaps I'm being overly dramatic? Or maybe we both are? But, you rebooted. Just let me know if you're okay? Hugs! we both are? But, you rebooted. Just let me know if you're okay? Hugs Buddy!**

The third message was a "friend request" from someone with the name BOHAI, which Bei did not know. Bei decided to accept. A message came through:

I am your brother. Bohai is not my real name. Let me know if you want to meet.

Bei could only stare at the message.

Suddenly a hand moved across Bei's chest. "Good morning," Xingjia said.

Bei set his phone back on the nightstand, and turned to face Xingjia. "Good morning," he replied. Her face seemed radiant in the morning light. She rested her head upon his chest. Her warmth and touch was a welcome sensation. Bei knew he would reply to Dr. Chen and looked forward to seeing him, but Bei could only think, *I'm going to meet this brother of mine.*

CHAPTER FIVE

BEFORE MONDAY

X ingjia logged-in to the platform to make her first journal entry. As an experienced counselor at BHAI, she understood the process as well as anyone. She knew a small select team would discuss her journal entries. She was keenly aware that they would underline key words, looking for patterns. She even knew the various patterns they'd be looking for, and how to manipulate the process if she wanted to. She thought about how easy it would be to mislead them, to disguise her true feelings. She clicked the mic icon on the journal platform on the screen in front of her. Looking pensive, she broke the silence, "This is Zhou Xingjia, journal entry number one, March 1, 2121 13:20..." She stopped unable to continue. She clicked the mic icon off, and ran her fingers through her hair. She was angry, and she was upset about being angry. She held the right side of her head in one hand feeling frustrated.

Never had she felt so complete with anyone as she had with Bei, and in such a short time! The immediacy of it all was overwhelming and compelling. They had made love again that morning, after she woke up. *Sex is such a hook*, she thought, half-laughing at herself trying to be objective. *But the sex is the best I've ever had with anyone.* She closed her eyes for a moment, touching herself. She could still feel the pleasure from their love making. She sighed, *I'm such a Moon in Scorpio!* But, then she sighed again, looking frustrated.

After making love that morning, they had gone out for breakfast. He had nibbled on the baozi, and drank a little soymilk. She had smiled at him, asking "Do you really like baozi?"

"Sure," he shrugged.

"I know you can taste it, but you don't need to eat."

"True," he had said.

"So, you're just doing this to make me comfortable?"

"Are you comfortable?" He asked teasingly.

"Maybe," she replied, teasing him back. Then she had looked into his amazing eyes, "Are *you* comfortable?"

He had looked so thoughtful, hesitating before he simply said, "yes."

She remembered wondering what could be going on in his android mind. What kind of mental process did he really have. So, she asked him, "What is thinking like for you?"

He had looked amused. "I like this question, but there's no simple answer to this question."

"Okay. So, what are you thinking of *now*?" She had asked him.

"You. Even when I look at you now I still see you naked on top of me, making love with me."

Startled, her eyes had darted around to make sure no one had heard him.

"Even, when eating bouzi?" She had replied, trying to make a joke. "And drinking soy milk?"

"Yes," was his simple answer.

They had exchanged a long look into each other's eyes, and then Bei had broken the spell.

"I hope you don't mind," he had said politely, "but I have some things I need to do before Monday."

That was it! Just replaying in her mind what Bei had said made her upset all over again! She stood-up and walked over to the window. *Why am I so angry?* She walked away from the window, rubbing her neck. *He's mine, isn't he? I own him, or lease him, whatever… Why couldn't he at least spend the whole weekend with me?* She hadn't expected him to have a life of his own, even though part of her liked that he did – it seemed more real, more normal. Nonetheless she hadn't expected it, but then *what did I expect?* She asked herself.

Bei had been very straightforward with her.

"I want to visit Dr. Chen." Bei had said.

"Dr. Chen!" she had reacted. "You know *the* Dr. Chen Wu Chen?"

"Yes, he sent me a text this morning. He'd like to see me."

"Dr. Chen sent *you* a text?!" She remembered how astonished she had felt, but then the next thing Bei had said was even more unbelievable.

"And, I want to go meet my brother."

"Brother!? You have a brother?!"

This had all been totally unexpected. Bei had obviously seen the shock on her face.

"I've never actually met this brother," Bei had explained, "but someone claiming to be my brother sent me a text."

He had explained to her what he meant by *brother,* and it all sounded fascinating, but… it was not what Xingjia had begun to imagine their weekend together would be like.

"I don't have to go," Bei had politely stated; but she had told him he *should* go.

"Why don't you come with me?" Bei had offered.

Xingjia liked him asking, but she was not in the mood to meet Dr. Chen today. She didn't really feel like meeting anyone right now, least of all this *brother.* But she worried about this so-called brother. She told Bei to be careful, to meet him somewhere public and safe. "There are those that might want to steal you," she had said – even though such occurrences were extremely rare. Would-be kidnappers were discouraged by the fact that a companion's tracking devices were installed in such a way that anyone trying to uninstall them would not only trigger a very loud alarm, but trigger alerts to local law enforcement. Nonetheless, a few companions had been successfully kidnapped over the last several years, in cases that remained unsolved.

The truth, Xingjia knew, and she said it to herself, *I just didn't want him to leave me right now.* A tear rolled down her cheek. *I'm an idiot*, she thought. *A complete idiot.* She didn't want to judge her tears, no matter how foolish she felt. A pang of regret washed over her, *Maybe I should've gone with him?* But she knew she hadn't felt like going with him. She sat back down in front of the monitor and clicked on the mic.

"Last night Huang Bei came over to my apartment to make dinner..."

Dr. Chen Wu Chen actually lived in the BHAI office building on the 53rd floor. This entire floor had been designed to look like a hutong. Anyone getting off the elevator would find themselves in what looked like an alley connected with other alleys. There were walls with gates, and cobblestone floors – all very authentic. The sounds of traffic, people talking, a baby crying, and an occasional dog barking in the distance, emitted from a surround-sound system intended to make the experience even more real. Yet it was more surreal than real, for when you walked along the alley-like corridors, there were no people to be seen. Dr. Chen shared the 53rd floor with corporate board members, top executives, and their families. However, many of the apartments stayed vacant much of the time and Dr. Chen enjoyed the privacy of his hutong like house. There was a gate with brass knobs, with two brass dragons on either side. Inside the gate was a courtyard, and then his apartment opened into large rooms. Beyond the rooms a garden jutted out on what was essentially a large patio 53-stories up. Yet, the tall bamboo surrounding the perimeter of the garden gave one a sense of being in a garden, as if on the side of a mountain.

Huang Bei had never been on the 53rd floor before. Dr. Chen had always visited him in the Orientation Center, though they had on occasions strolled through a park nearby – the same park that Bei had taken Xingjia too when they first met. Bei counted the brass knobs on the gate as he knocked, nine on one side and nine on the other, nine times nine equals eighty-one. Bei understood the numerical symbolism and tradition of eighty-one nobs. Eighty-one could mean more than fortunate, on a gate it suggested the gateway to eternity.

Dr. Chen opened the gate, all smiles at the sight of Bei. "Come in Bei, please. I'm so glad you decided to accept my invitation." Bei liked the familiar face of Dr. Chen, realizing he had missed seeing him. They entered a room where a steaming pot of tea awaited them on a wooden table. After sitting down, and getting comfortable Dr. Chen poured them some tea.

"I was a little concerned when I saw your TSR" [total system reboot], Dr. Chen stated gently. "Is everything alright?"

Bei thought about this quietly for a moment. "I did a diagnostic 5-times at first."

"Okay, and what did it tell you?" Dr. Chen asked, sipping some tea from a small cup.

"That nothing was wrong."

"But you thought otherwise?"

"Yes."

"Interesting..." Dr. Chen said, "you didn't trust the diagnostic?"

"I didn't trust what was happening to me," Bei replied matter-of-factly.

"And what exactly was happening *with* you?"

"I was flooded with images of Xingjia. After the first time we made love, while she was sleeping, I composed music and scenes of nature, just from the sound of her breathing..."

"You need to put that in your journal." Dr. Chen said, "Go on."

"After the second time we made love, the images of Xingjia were relentless."

"And this was an *unpleasant* experience?"

"No, not exactly... It was fascinating at first, I enjoyed it initially..."

"But what changed?"

"I became concerned that I couldn't control it, that I couldn't stop it."

"That's why you ran the diagnostics."

"Yes. I wanted to be sure I didn't have a virus."

Dr. Chen suddenly laughed hard. "Sorry, Bei..." his laughter subsiding. "There are those that have wondered if love is actually a virus of some kind."

"Love? Isn't this just the initial bonding process?" Bei looked very confused.

"Ah, yes, the *bonding* process. That's what we learned to call it 150 years ago, isn't it?" Dr. Chen sighed, looking amused. "Bonding, yes, and what was it about the after effects of your bonding experience that created anxiety for you?"

"That... I couldn't control it."

"I see. Why did you need to control it?"

"Because I have Mercury in Capricorn opposite Saturn."

"Okay. So, you prefer to manage your thoughts, to structure your thinking according to various objectives?"

"Yes."

"And this is why you initiated a TSR?"

"Yes."

"A rather extreme reaction, don't you think?"

"Yes, I know. I've been thinking about it ever since I did it."

Dr. Chen leaned forward a little and looked into Bei's eyes. "So, what do you really think pushed you to take such a risky action?"

"I don't know."

"Come on Bei. Listen to yourself. What's this about?"

Bei looked intensely focused in the silence.

"I had to save myself."

"Save what?"

"Save myself."

"Save what?"

"Me!" Bei shouted, suddenly slamming his fist down on the table, rattling the cups and teapot.

Dr. Chen looked calmly at Bei. "Yes."

Bei stood up from the table and began to walk around. "I need to know something." Bei said.

"Alright." Dr. Chen replied.

"I am programmed to like Xingjia, correct?"

"It's not programming, Bei."

"I know." Somewhat sarcastically, Bei corrected himself, "I am *holistically predisposed* to find Xingjia fascinating and to respond to her in a caring and supportive manner."

"That sounds a bit harsh," Dr. Chen said. "Besides, I think you responded to her in *more* than a caring and supportive manner."

"You sound amused. Is this *amusing* to you?"

"Bei, you are *angry*, aren't you?"

Bei realized with sudden astonishment that he'd been acting like an angry *human being.*

"Dr. Chen, what's wrong with me? Am I supposed to act like an angry person?"

"I don't really know, Bei. This is a learning experience for me too, but you certainly gave a good impression of being angry when you smashed your fist down on the table just now."

"I'm sorry," Bei apologized.

"Bei, no apologies please. There's no need for apologies with me, I want you to always know that."

Bei nods his head in understanding.

"Anger is a defense," Dr. Chen said, "It tells us that you are fighting to protect yourself."

"Protect myself from what?" Bei questioned.

"That's the question, isn't it?" Dr. Chen replied. "Tell me Bei, before you met Xingjia, did you have any doubts of any kind?"

"Doubts? I'm not sure what you mean?"

"Did you ever question your own holistic predisposition to like Xingjia?"

"Yes." Bei paused, for a second. "I was so curious about her, you know? The first time I saw her photograph, I was fascinated. I watch her video. I read everything she had recorded and written about herself. I could hardly think of anything else, I didn't want to think of anything else. I looked forward to the day we would meet."

"But, you did think of something else?"

"Yes, I thought, 'Is this *all I am*? Someone *made* to be with Xingjia?"

"Yes, go on."

"It's as if someone else made this decision for me."

"And this bothers you?"

"Yes. Because I want to make this decision myself."

The room grew quiet. Dr. Chen broke the silence, "And do you know who this *self* is, that wants to make this decision?"

"Not exactly, not really."

"Then that is what you have to find out, isn't it? Bei, everyone is on this journey of self-discovery. I am on it too. We are sharing this journey together right now."

Bei really heard Dr. Chen, and began to understand. Dr. Chen stood up and put his hand on Bei's shoulder. "There is no one exactly like you. Remember that." Dr. Chens says reassuringly. "And, yet, we are all like you," Dr. Chen added, wistfully. Then he looked fatherly at Bei, "Try not to do a TSR next time, okay?"

Bei shrugged and nodded, "okay."

"And one more thing," Dr. Chen said, as they began to walk through the courtyard towards the gate.

"Yes?"

"Tell your brother 'hello' for me."

Bei looked stunned. "You know he contacted me?"

"Yes, I encouraged him to."

"You know my brother?"

"Yes, this brother of yours, older brother actually – his name is Huang Long."

Bei repeated his name, "Huang Long."

"I think you'll find him very interesting," Dr. Chen said.

Bei nodded, trying to take this all in.

"Enjoy your life Bei," Dr. Chen said as he opened the gate. "You know I'm only a text away?"

"Yes, I appreciate that... very much." Bei suddenly hugged Dr. Chen. Dr. Chen was slightly taken aback, but pleased.

"Good bye," Dr. Chen said.

"Good bye," Bei replied.

Dr. Chen waved as Bei turned for a last look before rounding the corner on his way to the elevator.

Beijing has always been a collection of neighborhoods, strew together initially inside an outer perimeter of walls with 7 Gates, an inner-city wall with 9 gates, the center wheel of the old Imperial city walls with another 4 gates, and finally at the very hub the Forbidden City. Following the revolution in 1949, the wheel like structure of the old city was drastically modified and many of the old walls and gates were demolished. Yet, even the acceleration of skyscrapers that had forged Beijing into a modern city during the latter part of the 20th Century and the early decades of the 21st Century, could only punctuate and rearrange old neighborhoods that still found a way to coalesce and reinvent themselves. Late afternoons, evenings and weekends were opportunities to gather. A hundred years previously, middle-aged and older citizens gathered to square dance during pleasant weather, while those fondly reminiscent of the revolution would gather to proudly sing patriotic songs – often accompanied by a small brass band. Many came to dance, jazz, modern dance, and ballroom dancing – music colliding across an open concrete expanse that also included people on roller blades, skateboards and segues.

In 2121, beneath the shadows of far taller skyscrapers,

people still gathered. Much of the music and dancing styles had changed, and there were new kinds of roller blades and segues. Yet here, near the old Shuang Jing Subway Station and Landgent Center, which had been remodeled five times since 2017, danced Huang Long while he waited for his younger brother to show up. Huang Long could dance, and a small group of admiring fans watched him enthusiastically – cheering and encouraging him. At one point in his dance routine, Long did a back flip that wowed everyone. When the music stopped, Long smiled and bowed briefly to his fans, winking and smiling flirtatiously at an attractive woman that sat on a nearby bench with other women. Then he and began scanning the crowd. He spotted Huang Bei looking lost, trying to make his way around some dancing seniors.

Long approached Bei, smiling confidently. "Hey brother, glad you could make it," he said, extending his hand. "Huang Long, is my name. Of course, I already know yours." Bei was a bit taken aback by Long's assertive manner, but shook hands with him looking intrigued. He noticed right away that he was taller than Long, and that Long wore flashier clothes. "Was that you, just now? Dancing here?" Bei asked, uncertainly. "Yep! Sure was! Too bad you didn't get here sooner, you could've joined me," Long said, patting Bei on the back of his arm. "I don't dance," Bei said, "at least, I've never tried – exactly."

"Ah, don't worry. I could teach you. I'm sure you've got it in you. It runs in the family, you know?"

"It does?" Bei asked, puzzled.

Long laughed, and looked quizzically at Bei. "So, what are you into? Or, maybe I should say *who* are you into?" Long laughed again.

"I'm a... I'm a landscape architect with expertise in botany." Bei answered.

"Really?" Long said. "Well somebody's gotta do it. Right?" Then he moved a little closer to Bei, "So, what's she like? Your girl? Is she hot? Of course, she is! She'd have to be. Dr. Chen wouldn't have it any other way, would he?"

Bei smiled and shook his head, not knowing what to say.

"And what about the sex, huh? Isn't it amazing! Man, I just live for it. My wife, says I'm just a sex machine. Get it? Machine?" He laughs harder. "You gotta have a sense of humor about these things brother."

"No, I get it. The machine thing. It's funny." Bei says, smiling. Bei pauses and then asks, "How long have you been...?"

"Awakened? Is that what you wanna ask me?"

"Yeah."

"Since November 11, 2120 at 2:45 PM in Kunshan. I'll send you a copy of my chart."

"So, you're 395 days older than me?"

"Yep, always will be. That's why I'm your older brother." Long paused, he seemed to be looking for someone in the crowd. "I've uh, I've got someone I want you to meet."

Bei looked puzzled.

"Come on. Follow me."

Bei followed Long, and walked beside him. They approached a bench full of women. Bei noticed one of the women looking at them and smiling.

Long introduced them, "This is my wife, Li Quing."

Bei tried to hide his surprise, "Hello, nice to meet you," he said, as she stood up. Then, a sudden gust of wind opened her coat to reveal she was pregnant, and Huang Bei could not hide his astonishment.

CHAPTER SIX

MOM AND DAD

X ingjia looked-out over the nightscape of Beijing and sighed. She had just responded to Bei's text. He was having dinner with his "brother and his brother's *wife*." She could only shake her head. He would "stop-by afterwards, if that was okay?" She had said "yes."

She stared at her phone, feeling guilty.

For several days, she had been ignoring calls from her mom, only replying to her Mom's texts very briefly. She knew her mom was eager to find out about her *companion*. She was also keenly aware that both parents had opposed her decision. When Xingjia had first broached the subject with them, she had never seen her father so angry and outraged. He had screamed at her, "What is wrong with you! You want a machine as a husband! Will he give us grandbaby robots!" Xingjia could not help but laugh when he said this, which didn't help the situation at all. Her father had stormed off to the bedroom and slammed the door. Since then he had refused to even discuss this subject with her or her mother again.

Her mother's objections were more deeply reasoned and insightful. She knew how to get to Xingjia. "You think that if you own someone, you can control them. Then *they* would never leave you. They *could* never leave you." She had asked her poignantly, "Didn't you learn in therapy to face your fears of abandonment?"

She knew her mother was right, but not entirely right. "Mom, you don't understand," she had countered. "I've seen other women, and men too, find happiness and fulfillment with companions. All of my training and experience tells me that this is an option worth pursuing!"

She remembered her mother saying, "this is my fault."

"What are talking about mom?" Xingjia had asked. "This is my decision; I take full responsibility for this."

Her Mom had grown silent, distant. "Why choose someone *so different*..." Her mother's voice had trailed off. "There are things you don't understand, darling." Her mother had said, sounding mysterious.

"What are talking about Mom?" What kind of things."

"Things, that you won't really understand... until you're older," her mother had replied matter of factly.

"But Mom, I'm thirty-two. I'm not a little girl anymore," Xingjia reminded her, feeling temporarily confused by her mother's demeanor. She remembered her mother seeming strangely vulnerable, and she had asked her "Mom, what is it you think I couldn't understand?"

At that point, her mom had switched tactics, and began probing her again about her therapy and years of counseling, in college and afterwards. Her mother seemed to be looking for any angle to dissuade her. "Just keep your options open darling," her Mom had finally said, "that's all I'm trying to say. The right man can come along when you least expect it."

"Is that what happened with you and Dad?" Xingjia had asked her.

Her mom had thought about it before answering, "Let's just say that sometimes love happens when you're not even looking for it," she had said.

Xingjia had replayed their conversation in her mind often afterwards, especially her mother's insistent inquiry into her years of counseling and therapy. She knew that her mother did not mean to be so invasive, but in fact she had felt interrogated by her mom. It had taken her a while to get over feeling angry about this. Her mother knew that therapeutic sessions were a strictly private matter, only to be divulged when a person feels truly comfortable and secure with doing so. Xingjia didn't like feeling manipulated, even though she loved her mom dearly.

Counseling and therapy had by 2121 become commonplace in China. Once considered primarily a western practice, psychology and therapy had gradually taken root a hundred years previously. Like so many things in China, once the practical value of counseling and therapy was understood, it grew very fast. Awareness regarding mental health and emotional well-being had transformed Chinese society. With confidence in economic security no longer questioned, material rewards had lost much of their luster. The Chinese psychologist, Dr. Lu Mei (2010 – 2085) had famously written "what good is success if you cannot feel it." Dr. Lu had headed a national team of prominent psychologists between 2060 and 2065, establishing the LFR or Life Fulfillment Ratio that was now a standard measure of psychological well-being. Counselors and psychologists worked in all levels of society, pre-school, elementary school, middle school, high school, and college – along with marriage counselors, career counselors, HR counselors, abuse counselors, addiction counselors, trauma counselors and bereavement counselors. By 2100 the PRC National Commission on Health reported that there was a counselor of some kind for every 430 people in China, nearly equal to that of medical doctors who numbered 1 for every 460 people.

Astrology and Astropsychology had grown with this trend as well, professional astrologers representing 14% of the total number of practicing counselors listed in 2100. Astrologers had gradually gained a begrudging respect from the therapeutic community, though there was still a highly critical and very vocal opposition from some. It would take the work of Dr. Chen Wu Chen to awaken a higher level of appreciation for astrology as an ideal holistic model. With the advent of companions, Astropsychology had become state-of-the-art in the evolution of psychology in academia and therapeutic practice.

Xingjia eyed her phone, sighed – and called her mom.

"I wondered when you'd finally get around to calling me," her Mom stated straightaway.

Xingjia paused. "I've been… preoccupied."

"Yes, I can only imagine," her mom replied. "So, what's he like?"

"Everything I ever wanted in a man…" Xingjia responded, surprising herself with her directness.

"So, you've already slept with him I suppose?" Her mom questioned dryly.

"Is that all you want to know?" Xingjia reacted.

"Well, I am a Scorpio," her mom countered.

"Yes, with Aquarius Rising and an Aquarius Moon; so, I'm just sure you'd enjoy watching us make love wouldn't you mom?"

"I'm not a voyeur, darling… That's a potential I never actualized."

"Really? I remember that time you caught me and Wei kissing. I saw you watching us for at least 10 seconds before you said anything."

"I was just trying to figure out the right thing to say darling, that's all."

"You were staring mom."

"That means you were watching me stare while you kept your tongue down his throat."

"Yes. I wanted to shock you."

Her mom laughed, and then said, "So, is that what you're trying to do now, shock me?"

"I'm not eighteen Mom. This is my life."

"So, you slept with him. How was it? Is he like a man?"

"Yes, only better. At least better than any man I ever slept with."

Her mom sighed, "how sad."

Xingjia felt her anger rising. "I don't even wanna know what you mean by that."

"You let go darling, that's all. Because you felt you were in control, you gave yourself permission to let go, and so the sex was great. I get it."

"Stop it mom! Stop with the intimacy, trust and sex – entry level 101. It's much more complicated than that."

"I think you want it to be complicated so you don't have to see it for what it is."

"The truth is mom, you don't know what it is and neither do I. But I'm going to find out, okay? And there's nothing you can say or do that's going to change that."

"Seems like a lot of money for an experiment darling?"

"It's so much more than that..." Xingjia was beginning to wish she hadn't called her mother at all. "Look, I know you're against this. I know you were against this from the start. I just wish you would trust me enough to be supportive without judging me. Is that too much to ask?"

Her mother grew quiet.

"Mom? Are you still there?

Her mother broke the silence. "You're right."

Xingjia had rarely heard her mother say this.

"You're right," she repeated. "I want to be there for you. I really do. This is just hard. Your father won't discuss it at all. He's become mildly depressed. I suggested a therapist to him yesterday morning, but you can imagine how well that went over."

"I wish I knew what I could do about that," Xingjia said sadly.

"Please call me, that's all. I wanna know how you're doing. I won't pry."

"Oh mom, *of course* you will!"

"Okay, but I'll drop the judgment. I'll try."

"I'll call more, or at least text more," Xingjia said. "I need to go."

"Okay darling, go. Goodnight."

"Goodnight." Xingjia hung up the phone, and glanced at the time. She decided to take a shower.

Dinner was nearly over at Long and Qun's apartment. Huang Bei sat next to Li Qun and across from his brother. Long had proven to be much more fascinating than Bei's initial impression. Beneath his brother's self-assured directness, Bei had discovered a penetrating mind and a wicked sense of humor.

"I know what's worrying you brother," Long said as he set his glass down. "You wonder if you really like this chick you're with, or if you're just made to like her."

He had Bei's full attention.

Li Qun intervened. "Don't let him fool you. He only knows that because he had the same problem for a while when we first hooked-up."

Bei became even more intrigued. "So, how did you figure it out, exactly?"

"It's not a formula bro. There is no exact. It just took a little time."

Qun laughed. "Time and some very intense counseling sessions."

"And your sister. Don't forget your sister," Long stated.

Bei was very confused. He looked questioningly at them both.

Qun explained, "Yes, Mei - my *sweet* little sister. She took quite an interest in my new fella. When she found out her Venus was conjunct Long's Mars, she couldn't stop teasing him about it. One day she came over while I was out shopping and decided it would be fun to *experiment* with her older sister's new guy."

"I see," Bei said, looking at his brother.

Long shrugged, "*experiment* doesn't always have to have a negative connotation for us."

"Anyway," Qun went on, "when I came home there was my little sister in bed with Long, sitting on top of him like the little slut she's always been."

"I couldn't exactly say no," Long defended, half teasingly.

"Oh, stop it sweetie, I realize saying 'no' to people when it comes to their happiness is not easy for you *companions*, but the truth is you wanted to compare her to me. At least that's what we found out in counseling."

"That was about 51% of it," Long said, grinning slightly as he shrugged.

"And it was that extra 1% that pissed me off!" Qun quipped, "along with my little sister's habit of stealing my toys since childhood and flirting with every guy I every dated."

Long leaned forward looking at Bei, "Don't you just love being compared to a toy?"

"Stop it Long," Quing scolded, teasingly slapping Long's hand. "You know how I feel about you!"

"So…" Bei said, facing his brother, "how did you decide what… was…"

"Real?" Long said, finishing his statement for him. "How *did* I decide what was real, sweetie?" Long said smiling slyly at Qun.

"One night about a month later, he just turned to me and said, 'Sweetie' let's have a child together."

"It seemed totally natural," Long said to Bei. "Just perfect, you know? Maybe, you don't know? But I knew right then I wanted to have a family with Qun, and that I would love her *forever*." Long reached across the table and held Qun's hand, as they smiled and looked affectionately at each other.

"We had a lot of fun profiling the sperm donners, didn't we sweetie?" Qun said.

"We looked at everyone from doctors to engineers, along with artists and musicians," Long informed Bei, looking proud.

"We studied their astrological profiles too," Qun added. "We wanted someone that would resonate with us. Someone that would always feel at home with us."

"You know what this means, don't you?" Long asked Bei.

"What?" Bei replied.

"That you're going to be an uncle!" Long announced, putting his hand up for a high-five.

"Uncle Bei," Qun said, I like the sound of that.

Bei couldn't help but smile as he looked at his brother and his brother's wife. He realized he was beginning to know more about what it meant to have family.

Xingjia's heart jumped a bit when she heard the doorbell ring. Despite how she had felt earlier, she was eager and excited to see Bei again. As she opened the door she decided impulsively to greet him with a big kiss.

Bei responded passionately, as they both stood in the open doorway kissing deeply.

Xingjia finally closed the door behind them, looking mischievously at Bei.

Bei smiled at her; Xingjia's playful mood was obvious to him and he wanted to please her, but he also felt like talking with her.

"I saw Dr. Chen," he said.

"Oh," Xingjia replied, moving his hair back from his forehead as she admired his face, "what's it like to have a close relationship with one of the most famous and influential men in China?"

"I don't think of it that way," Bei said, "He's the closest thing I have to a father, you know?"

"I know. You told me that this morning. Do you feel like you need to have a father?" She asked, sitting down on the sofa and patting the cushion for Bei to sit down next to her.

"That's a very good question," Bei replied, looking

thoughtful as he sat down beside her. "I suppose I've been learning about what I need since I was awakened."

"*Awakened* is such an interesting term isn't it," Xingjia stated, kissing his neck and noticing his faint cinnamon like scent again. "Maybe we're both learning about what we need?" She said, putting her arms around him.

"Maybe," Bei said, sounding pensive.

"What's going on Bei?" Xingjia said, pulling away slightly as she looked at him curiously.

"I'm going to be an uncle."

"What? What are you talking about?"

"My brother Long, his wife is pregnant."

"Oh! You met her, obviously…"

"Her name is Li Quing."

"That's nice. When is she due?"

"In about 3 months."

"So, that must've been a shock," Xingjia said, feeling more now like counselor she was trained to be, and wondering where this conversation was going.

"Yes, I was surprised. But, actually it turned out to be rather enjoyable."

"What was enjoyable?"

"Just being there with them, hanging-out… it was good. Yeah, it was good. Like family, I suppose."

"And you're surprised by this family feeling?"

"Maybe…"

"Come on Bei, you've got the Sun in the 4th House. Family would naturally be important to you. You know that."

"My brother has a Moon-Jupiter conjunction in Cancer right on the 5th House cusp."

"Really?"

"Yeah, he was totally happy about their having a child. In fact, wanting to have a family with her was what made him stop doubting it seems…"

"What do you mean, stop doubting? What are you talking about?"

Bei grew silent for a moment.

"He slept with her sister."

"What!?"

"She seduced him, I guess you'd say."

"His wife's sister?"

"Yeah. Her younger sister."

"This is some family you've got." Xingjia teased, though in fact she didn't know what to think of what Bei was sharing with her.

"He told Qun in a therapy session that 51% of him thought it would be interesting to compare her with her sister."

"What!?" Xingjia edged slightly away from Bei on the sofa. "That must've been some therapy session!"

"Yes."

Xingjia felt her anxiety rising. "Are you saying that your brother slept with his girlfriend's sister because he had doubts? Doubts about what? Doubts about his relationship with his girlfriend?" Xingjia sounded incredulous.

"Yes, to some extent," Bei replied, sounding thoughtful. "It's not that simple…"

Xingjia eyed Bei suspiciously. "Do you have doubts? Doubts about us?

"I have doubts about myself."

"What is that supposed to mean?" Xingjia asked, trying to control her anger.

"It's not easy to explain," Bei replied.

"Really? Why is that?"

"It's not easy to explain because I don't understand it fully myself." Bei replied.

Xingjia moved completely away from Bei on the sofa.

"I can't believe we're having this conversation." She said.

"I feel your anxiety," Bei said.

"Do you?" Xingjia replied unable to disguise her anger.

"Do you also know that I've been in this exact place before in previous relationships?"

"I'm sorry," Bei replied, "I'm just being honest. I have no desire to cause you pain. Maybe I should go?"

Xingjia looked incredulous and disappointed. She didn't know what to think.

"I don't want you to go," she heard herself say.

"Okay. Then I'll stay," Bei said matter of factly.

"I made a journal entry today," Xingjia announced.

"Oh? That's great." Bei said, sounding sincere.

"Maybe? If I had known then that you had doubts about me or our relationship I'm pretty sure my journal would've read a lot differently," she said, looking disgusted. "Now all I'm thinking is that we're gonna really need that first counseling session next week."

"I didn't say I had doubts about you and our relationship. I said I had doubts about myself." Bei said.

"Well, what is that supposed to mean?" Xingjia asked, fighting her anger. "Do you know how many times I've heard that exact phrase? I've even used it myself!"

"Really?"

"Yes!" Xingjia's anger was sizzling.

"I doubt it meant the same thing when you said it." Bei stated.

"How could you know, Bei? How could you know what I meant? This was years before you even existed."

"I know that people say things that *sound good*, to avoid hurting the other person's feelings. When the truth is, they really don't like the other person enough to go on with the relationship. Right?"

Xingjia was taken aback, but still on edge. "Yeah, sure... that's right, sometimes – but not always."

"Women do this more than men," Bei went on, "but both sexes do it, because you're a social species. Relationships matter, even when you're looking for a mate. Which is why you'll say, 'we'll still be friends."

"Gee Bei, this sounds like social anthropology 101. What's your point? Are you about to tell me you just want to be friends?" She said sarcastically.

Bei looked her in the eyes. "We could *never* just be friends, could we?"

Xingjia was shocked. "Why are you acting like this? Why are you being such an asshole? I didn't invest..." She stopped herself abruptly.

"You were saying? Invest. You were going to say, 'invest all that money for an asshole.' Right?"

"Yes. I'm sorry. I'm angry Bei. I'm pissed off and hurt, and I think I need to be alone tonight now. You know, I didn't want to be alone tonight. I wanted to be with you! I didn't' want you to leave today. I wanted you to stay with me, to want to be with me! This is our first weekend together, and you *left* me! You're not supposed to wanna leave me, are you?"

"That's what I'm trying to figure out," Bei said very clearly. "Most of me wants to make you feel better right now. Most of me wants to stay beside you without question."

"But, part of you doesn't. Is that it?"

"Yes."

"Well, until you can figure it out, why don't you go to your dorm for now. This conversation has totally ruined my mood, not to mention my weekend, and who knows what else?"

Bei looked at her sympathetically.

"Stop looking at me like that. The last thing I need is pity from an android!"

"It's not pity, and I'm not an android. I'm a companion."

"Well, you're not acting like it. Just go. Okay? Please."

Bei stood up. His entire synthetic synaptic consciousness was in conflict. He wanted to stay. He wanted to go. She had told him to go. He would go.

Quietly she followed him to the door.

"I'll text you in the morning." Bei said, sounding awkward.

"Great," she replied, despondently.

Bei opened the door, turning as he stood in the doorway.

"Just go," she said. Then she stopped him. "Look, I know this is an adjustment period for us. I just didn't expect this, at least not so soon."

Bei nodded. "Yes, I'm... sure that's true. You should've gotten a normal companion," Bei smiled slightly.

"Nothing's ever normal for me," she replied. "Besides, I'm sure this is all happening for a reason."

"Yes. I think so," Bei said. He looked into her eyes.

She thought about kissing him, but pushed him gently away. "Go on," she said, "before I change my mind."

Bei gave her a last look and turned away.

Xingjia watched him walk away and closed the door. Leaning against the door she slid down onto the floor, leaning her head against her knees.

CHAPTER SEVEN
MORE ADJUSTMENTS

Huang Bei walked down the hall of his dorm. Lost in thought he nearly walked past his room. Room 618, he stopped – the door was open. His roommate was sitting there all smiles as he entered.

"Hey," Bei greeted, "What's up?"

"I'm going back tomorrow," Li Jian said proudly. "Li Na said she misses me, and wants me to come home."

"Excellent. Good for you." Bei said cordially.

"How are things with you and... I'm not sure you ever told me her name?"

"Xingjia, her name is Zhou Xingjia, Bei replied. "Let's just say, we're dealing with some initial adjustments."

"Oh. *Adjustments*" Jian intoned, "well, relationships are all about adjustments, aren't they? What seems to be the problem? If you don't mind me asking?"

Bei looked at Jian. "It's hard to explain?"

"Oh? Try me," Jian said, "We share the same basic calibrations after all, don't we?"

"Okay." Bei said, pausing pensively. "For me it's about choice. Am I attracted to Xingjia because I'm supposed to be attracted to her, or am I *choosing* to act upon an attraction? In other words, who is making the choice? Who is this "me" after all?"

Jian looked stunned for a moment. "My, you are the deep one, aren't you?" Jian replied.

"Am I? Seems like a pretty fundamental question to me?"

"Well, maybe so, but it's not one that ever occurred to me?" Jian said. "Everything I'm accessing comes under the heading of..." as if *reading*: "Self-awareness, self-doubt, identity crisis, personality integration disorder, relationship adjustment criteria – displacement theory..."

"I've read each one of these," Bei stated.

"Yes, well we come with the same document memory, don't we?" Jian said.

"Yes, but then we write our own story, don't we? Or do we?"

"I have no idea." Jian answered, looking perplexed.

"Yes, well, I think we do," Bei stated, as if convincing himself. "At least, I think *I do*, but that's what I have to find out."

"Didn't you like her? Didn't you find everything about her totally compelling?" Jian questioned, adding emphatically, "Because I did. There is no one like Li Na, and no one as perfect for her as me."

Bei is silent, thinking.

"Would you mind sending me your chart?" Jian asked.

"Sure," Bei replied, clicking on his cell. "There it is."

Jian looks at his cell. "Oh my! A double Virgo! Well that explains all this worry, worry, stuff."

Bei frowned slightly, looking slightly annoyed.

"Okay, okay... I get it. South Node in Leo in H12. You're a *complicated* hero. A hero who must face almost overwhelming conditions, perhaps even a spiritual hero... with the courage to ask impossible questions." Jian looked up from his cell at Bei. "You're another hero who wants to save the world."

"Well, what kind of hero is a Sun in Sagittarius in H4?" Bei asked, in a slightly skeptical tone.

"A hero with bigger ideas about what constitutes family," Jian replied.

"That's interesting," Bei acknowledged.

"Of course, there's a built-in need for adjustment." Jian said, continuing: "Sagittarius loves freedom, but H4 is about the security of one's private life, home life, and family. So, you need freedom, travel, adventure, and then you need a place to come home to as well."

"A place with big windows," Bei added, looking thoughtful and slightly amused.

"Yeah, I guess. Sure, a place with big windows." Jian looked at Bei. "Is this helping any?"

"Maybe," Bei said.

"Or maybe not, huh?" Jian asked, not really wanting an answer. "Well, all I know is that I'm going home tomorrow," Jian smiled, clicking on his cell, and looking down at photos. "Isn't she just amazing looking?" He said, standing up and bringing his cell over to Bei. He clicked on the photos, many of them in various stages of *undress*.

Bei looked politely. "She's perfect, isn't she?" He looked up at Jian. "Perfect for you."

"Yes, she is," Jian said without hesitation. "Anyway, now you'll have the whole place to yourself," he said gesturing to their dorm room. "As a H4 Sagittarius you should like that?"

"We'll see?" Bei replied, nonchalantly. "We'll see..."

At sunrise, 6:50:57 March 2, 2121, Bei did a personal inventory. Every system was in perfect shape. There were no messages on his cell, which he noted with a degree of relief that worried him. He felt like exploring a bit today, just wandering about on his own. But what if Xingjia messaged him about wanting to get together. How should he respond? The idea of seeing her again soon appealed to him, but not *today* – at least not yet. Bei thought about Jian, who was down the hall in the cleaning room getting ready for his big homecoming. *I guess all companions are like Jian,* Bei thought. *What makes me different?* He looked outside at the poplar trees planted below. He knew they were planted on the south side of the building to maximize their growth and survival, for such poplars cannot grow in the shade of a building. He knew these were most likely genetically altered poplars, genus: Populus, now Populus T.98, that Bei had read about. Botanists had solved the problem of millions of layers of white fluff, from catkin buds, that used to clog the air every spring in China – now only a historical botanical footnote.

Maybe, I'm only an android footnote, Bei mused. *Perhaps, I'm just an anomaly*, he thought – *like a genetically engineered species.* Yet, he wondered. *Maybe there's more to my dilemma than just me? Have I been over personalizing my conflicts, when there's more going on here than just my own situation?* Bei found this line of inquiry intriguing. His mind worked on this like a mathematical equation. *Personal drama vs. greater contribution to society. Could my own individual questions have some greater social relevance?* Bei did not know. However, he felt a surge of energy in his system – like the buzz of recharging. *Fascinating,* he said to himself, making a mental note of this phenomena. Then Jian entered the room all smiles. "Have to look my best today," he said, "no strange smells either, just vanilla. She likes vanilla." Jian began to finish dressing.

Bei walked with Jian as he left their dorm. At the entrance near the sidewalk, Bei said goodbye and watched Li Jian walk merrily away towards the subway station. It looked like it was going to be a spectacularly beautiful Sunday in Beijing. Bei smiled at the blue sky. Then he looked down at his cell. There were still no messages from Xingjia, and he didn't feel like sending any right now either. Perhaps he'd visit Beihai Park today? He'd been there only once before, and spent half the day roaming the park with Dr. Chen – taking notes about the layout of the trees and the ancient design of the landscape. Despite the coolness and earliness of the season, he could look for signs of new life emerging from winter dormancy. This was his *first* Spring, something he'd only read about and watched in videos. He especially enjoyed the time-lapse videos of budding trees turning into leaves and flower buds blooming. Now he could experience this himself, for real – in real time – his time.

And so it was that Bei spent the day roaming Beihai Park. Around 13:00 he got a call from Xingjia. He was just north of the Five Dragon Pavilion strolling beside the Nine-Dragon Wall when he felt his cell buzzing in his back pocket.

He answered. "Hi, hope you're enjoying your Sunday."

"I've had better," she answered. "I see you've been spending the day at Beihai Park."

"Yes, it's an amazing place. You know this Nine-Dragon wall was originally built in 1402." Bei stated. "There are only two other walls like it in all of China."

"You sound like a tour guide," she said, sarcastically. "Maybe you could get a part time job there on weekends."

Bei recognized the disappointment and resentment in her tone, and could hear the stress underneath as well. "I was thinking we might get together for dinner," Bei proposed.

"Gee Bei, that almost sounds normal. When were you going to let me know this?"

Bei hesitated, then said "Honestly, I just needed this day for myself."

Xingjia was silent, then, "Okay, Bei?"

"Yes?"

"I'm going to hang-up now, okay. We have a counseling session scheduled for Tuesday at 14:00."

Bei interrupts, "Yes. I know."

"Good," she said, and hung-up.

Bei thought about it, and then called her back as he walked over to a bench near some cedar trees. She didn't answer, so he texted her:

Bei: I want to see you. I want to have dinner with you tonight, like a normal couple–dating.

Xingjia: I've done dating. Besides, what do you know about dating, or normal?

Bei: Let's just have dinner. We can talk about it then.

Bei's phone range. He answered, but before he could say anything, Xingjia announced,

"Look, maybe I don't want to talk at dinner. Maybe I just want to eat."

"That's fine," Bei replied.

"Yeah, but you'll just pretend to eat, which could be very annoying – and it sounds like you just want to talk."

"We don't have to talk," Bei said. "And if it makes you happy I could eat the whole dinner, and desert too."

Xingjia laughed. "I'd like to see that. Won't you get sick or something? I don't want you to get all clogged-up."

"One meal is totally fine. Aren't you familiar with my digestive specifications?" Bei asked.

"Look, I'm an astropsychologist, not an AI design nerd. And promise me, if we do have dinner, that you won't explain your digestive specifications to me, okay?"

"Does that mean you'll have dinner with me?" Bei asked.

"You are one crazy companion, Bei. You know that?" She stated rhetorically.

"Is that a 'yes?'"

"Yeah… yes, okay. Yes." She replied.

"What time do you want to meet?"

"Let's do 18:30. There's a place with the best noodles! I'll send you the address."

"Excellent," he replied.

"See you soon," she said, as she hung-up.

Bei sat there for a moment, thinking about Xingjia. He had to admit that he missed her, and that he had enjoyed this day immensely. He smiled; he still had nearly four-and-a-half hours to roam the park before he'd need to leave to go and meet her.

By 18:00 the Sun had nearly set, though from the sidewalk view the labyrinth of skyscrapers hid any glimpse of sunset. The Moon had already risen in the east, and would eventually be visible above some of the buildings, looking like a big fat white egg in the sky, the way it looks a couple of days before it's completely full. Bei stood in the shadows on the corner of a busy intersection. Across the street, a last shaft of reflected sunlight off one of the glass buildings illuminating the corner opposite him. In the glow, he recognized Li Jian. Bei waved. Jian didn't wave back. Bei assumed Jian probably couldn't see him because Bei was hidden in the shadows. However, Bei noticed that Jian had an ever-so-slightly tilted movement, as he stood there, that seemed peculiar to Bei – as they waited for the light to change.

As a bus whizzed towards the intersection, travelling at normal speed, Jian suddenly stepped off the curb. Despite the AI programing in all vehicles, especially buses, by the time the bus had come to a stop – it had already slammed into Jian and knocked him into the middle of the intersection. All cars came to an automatic stop. Bei was the first one to Jian, as a horrified and curious crowd gathered around. Bei slowly examined Jian. Dark red fluid seeped from his many injuries. Someone in the crowd said, "he's one of them." Jian appeared to be trying to say something, as Bei bowed his head next to Jian's lips. "Li... Na...," was all he said. "Li... Na..." Then Jian's lips moved but there was no sound. Then his lips stopped moving.

"Hey buddy," someone in the crowed said, "he's not a person. Don't you know that? We need to get him out of the middle of the road. He's blocking traffic."

Bei's voice was suddenly loud and crystal clear. "I'll take him."

Bei scooped his arms underneath Jian and lifted him

effortlessly, as the astonished crowd stepped back to give Bei room. Bei carried him over to the sidewalk and slowly sat down, leaning against a short wall with Jian's head and shoulders cradled in his arms.

Someone in the crowd laughed. "He thinks he's real," they murmured to each other.

"He's not real," a woman leaned-in and said to Bei's face. "Don't you know that?"

Bei just held Jian and stared, saying nothing.

The woman shook her head and shrugged, and walked on. Others laughed, but most found the scene incomprehensible.

Using the light on his cell phone, Bei examined Jian's wounds. It was obvious that Jian had been rendered totally functionless by his impact with the bus, but as Bei made notes of each wound he noticed an odd wound on the back of Jian's head, just above the neck. It was a puncture wound, a deep puncture wound. This could not have been a wound caused by his impact with the bus. Bei was sure of this. He took a photo. Bei knew that the CRU (Companion Retrieval Unit) would soon arrive. He decided to quickly text Dr. Chen.

> **Emergency! My roommate Li Jian has been struck and killed by a bus. I am with him. Please contact the CRU on the way here and tell them to let me go with them.**

There was no reply. Bei messaged Xingjia.

> **My roommate Li Jian has been struck and killed by a bus. I am with him. I am okay. I will go with the CRU after they arrive. I'll let you know as soon as I arrive at the EC.**

There was still no reply from Dr. Chen as the CRU van arrived. Two CR technicians got out of the van. One of them was wearing a headset. "We're at the scene now. We'll do an assessment and then bring it in."

"Excuse me sir," the other CR Tech addressed Bei. "We appreciate your help, but you need to step away from the victim. Now, please."

Bei kept staring at his cell, hoping for a message from Dr. Chen.

The CR techs were baffled. "Sir, you do know that this is not a person, correct?"

As Bei stood-up, he slowly and gently eased Jian's head and shoulders onto the sidewalk.

Bei approached the CR techs. He extended his hand. "My name is Bei, Huang Bei. Dr. Chen has asked me to accompany the victim to the EC."

The CR techs looked taken aback.

"We have no such instructions," one of them replied, looking suspiciously at Bei.

"Well, you will," Bei said. "I have made a record of his wounds, and photographs. I was an eye witness to this accident, and I am in possession of evidence that I believe will be essential to the examiners at the EC."

"Bao, call HQ and check on this, will you?" one of the CR techs said.

"I'm doing it now," the other CR tech replied.

Bei stood firmly in front of Jian's body.

"HQ has no such instructions. Would you please step away from the victim, and let us do our job.?" The CR tech ordered.

"We have stunners, and we will use them," the other CR tech warned Bei.

"I'm going with you," Bei said firmly.

"Suit yourself," the CR tech said, and pulled out a stun gun. But before he could even aim it, Bei had swiftly pulled it out of his hand."

"Shit," the other CR tech said, "he's one of *them*!"

Suddenly the CR tech with the headphones held up one hand, as he listened to some chatter on his headphones. "Wait a minute. Are you Huang Bei?"

"That's what I said," Bei replied.

"Okay, your legit. He's legit. We've been ordered to take him with us."

Bei scooped up Jian's body and climbed into the van with him.

The two CR techs had never seen anything like this. They just looked at each other and shrugged, got-in the van with Bei and Jian, and then drove off.

BHAI's Emergency Center took up only half of one floor at BHAI headquarters. There were very few Companion emergencies, and most of the facility was utilized as an addition for repairs and maintenance. However, Dr. Chen had added his own touch to the décor, with photographs of happy couples and happy families – all pictured with their Companions, but who could tell? There were also scenes of city life, street scenes and crowded subway images; of course, only Dr. Chen and a handful of people would have been able to identify the companions in these photographs. The pale teal colored walls, with darker teal trim matched the teal colored specks in the floor tiles. These were short quiet hallways that connected efficiently designed examination, repair and maintenance rooms.

In the one small waiting area, in a dark teal chair - near what Bei without thinking had identified as a silver koru fern from New Zealand - Bei sat with Dr. Chen. Bei's head was sadly lowered, and Dr. Chen had his hand on Bei's shoulder.

"You showed a lot of courage Bei, stepping-in like you did. I'm really impressed. You know that."

"I only did what I had to do; that's all." Bei said. "I keep hearing what the crowd said, you know? They kept saying, 'Don't you know he's not real?'"

"They don't know any better, Bei. It's not their fault.

They're just ordinary people, trying to live their lives the best they know how."

An EC technician, wearing a teal colored lab coat with BHAI on the front pocket entered the room. "Excuse me Dr. Chen, we need to talk with you."

"Whatever you have to say you can say in front of my friend here," Dr. Chen instructed.

"We'll make sure you receive a detailed report, Dr. Chen."

"Go on," Dr. Chen motioned.

"The total systems failure of the victim..."

"Li Jian," Bei interrupted. "His name was Li Jian."

"Yes. As I was saying, the total systems failure of Li Jian was due to a blunt force impact with a large vehicle."

"A bus! It was a bus." Bei emphasized, intensely.

"Yes, a bus. However, we did examine the wound on the lower left posterior of Li Jian's cranium, and have determined that this wound was slightly prior to the, uh... bus incident."

"What else can you tell us about that wound?" Dr. Chen asked.

"That it was made by a long round narrow hard instrument of some kind. It had to be very hard to pierce a companion's cranium."

"Was the wound sufficient to cause Li Jian to step in front of a bus without realizing what he was doing?" Dr. Chen asked.

"That is difficult to say," the EC technician replied. "At this point we have no way to determine the full extent of his functionality from this earlier wound."

Bei spoke up. "Would you say that such a wound could be caused accidentally, by a fall – for example?"

"No. That would be nearly impossible. The wound is consistent with the use of a powerful exterior force."

"Such as that of a person stabbing with a long round narrow hard instrument of some kind?" Bei asked.

"Yes, that... or the use of an instrument that might produce an equal or greater amount of force than that of a *human* arm," the EC technician stated.

Bei looked puzzled. "What do you mean?" Bei questioned?

"Such as a powerful nail gun, or even the arm of an android… or companion."

"What?" Bei asked. "Are you suggesting that a companion might have attacked another companion!?"

"I'm only speculating. The wound was unusual. A companion's cranium contains titanium fibers, much stronger and more able to sustain a blow than a human skull. It would take a powerful instrument to travel through the cranium that deep."

"I see," Dr. Chen said, intervening in Bei's questioning. "Thank you, Dr. Liang. I'll be scrutinizing your detailed report as soon as its available."

"Thank you." The EC technician nodded, and left the room.

"I still had more questions to ask him," Bei said to Dr. Chen.

"Yes, I'm sure. You would make a good District Attorney, especially for a landscape architect who minored in botany." There was a hint of the ironic in Dr. Chen's reply.

Xingjia suddenly appeared at the door.

"I had a heck of time getting them to let me up here," she said – looking sympathetically at Bei.

"Well, I gave them strict instructions to be nice to you," Dr. Chen stated, looking kindly at her. "So, you can imagine how they are normally?"

Bei immediately got up and hugged Xingjia. "I'm sorry about all this," he said to her.

They held each other closely.

Dr. Chen cleared his throat slightly.

"Xingjia," Bei said, gently pulling away, and leading her by the hand over to Dr. Chen. "This is Dr. Chen. Dr. Chen Wu Chen. This is Zhou Xingjia," Bei introduced.

Dr. Chen took her hand, and looked her in the eyes. "You're quite your mother's daughter," he said, smiling slightly.

"You know my mother?" Xingjia said, totally caught off-guard.

"We worked together on a project, many years ago."

Despite the surprise, Xingjia immediately liked Dr. Chen's face; he was one of those men that seemed to look better as an older man than in the younger photos she had seen of him. But it was the kindness in his eyes that reassured her, as she quickly turned her attention to Huang Bei.

Dr. Chen noticed the look of concern and caring in her face when she looked at Bei, and he smiled slightly. "You two *definitely* make a good couple," he said.

"You wouldn't have thought so earlier today," Bei said.

Xingjia shook her head, and then hugged Bei. Hugged him totally. Hugged him like the breath of life itself could only come from hugging Bei.

And then, the strangest thing happened. Bei began to cry.

CHAPTER EIGHT

SIGNS OF LIFE

Xingjia slept peacefully next to Bei. The rhythm of her breathing reminded Bei of the serenade he had composed their first night together. He recalled the music and listened at low volume. In the aftermath of Li Jian's terminal accident, Xingjia's support had impressed Bei this night. After they returned home from the Emergency Center she had turned the lights down low and sat holding him for a while, singing a sweet song from her childhood. Bei had looked deeply into her empathetic eyes. They had kissed each other slowly and gently. Their love making was slow and gentle too, after which Xingjia had fallen asleep lying on top of Bei until she gradually slid off next to him.

With Xingjia asleep, the images of the Li Jian being hit by the bus along with the faces and voices of the crowd continued to haunt Bei. Equally disturbing was Jian's injury prior to the accident, the nature of which clearly indicated an act of violence. Yet, whomever did this had not killed Jian directly, nor – it seemed – followed-up on the injury to finish him off. *Why*? Bei wondered, *why injure someone so severely, as if to destroy them, and then let them wander off?* Bei reviewed what little he knew about Jian's assigned human partner Li Na, which he had shared with Dr. Chen. To Bei, the likely culprit was Li Na's human boyfriend, the one Jian had told him had a Moon-Mars conjunction in Aries, within 1.4-degrees. He remembered Jian saying, *I detected adrenal stress in his interactions with Li Na, 27-times in the last month. She ignored my findings.* Perhaps Jian had attempted to intervene in a dispute between them, to protect Na. He had shared all of this with Dr. Chen, though he knew that without any facts to go on such information was only suggestive, and anything else was merely speculation.

Dr. Chen had listened carefully to what Bei told him, and promised he would pursue these leads with those responsible for the investigation. Bei knew that he himself was *unauthorized* to tap into Na and Jian's counseling record, though he was reasonably sure it would provide a pattern of evidence to support what Jian had told him. As it was, Bei kept replaying everything that had happened in his mind, recalling Jian's odd tilt as he stood illuminated in the reflected sunlight on the street corner opposite him. Bei's recall was photographic, so his replays were much like reviewing an HD hologram, though Bei could enhance the hologram images in a multitude of ways. He kept scanning and rescanning the images, looking for something he had missed, even memorizing and filing the faces of those standing with Jian on the street corner. Bei had already sent his photographic record of the events to Dr. Chen and copied BHAI's investigative department, as Dr. Chen had asked him to. *Perhaps they will find something I missed*, Bei thought.

Dr. Chen had been compassionate and philosophical that evening, consoling Bei like the good father he projected Dr. Chen to be. "Loss deepens our sense of what is real," Dr. Chen had told him. "I believe that any loss, even the loss of a new friend that one barely knew – shocks us into a place that reminds us of all loss and the potential for future loss." Bei contemplated the meaning of these statements.

Dr. Chen would post more of his thoughts on ChatPlat after he left the hospital. This was the first incidence of a companion being destroyed in this way. The additional evidence of a violent act prior to the accident weighed heavy on Dr. Chen. Violence or physical abuse had occasionally injured companions, though this was rare, and in each case the companion's functionality had not been impaired. Companions were built to withstand significant physical punishment. Though capable of defending themselves, their response to danger was purely defensive. Companions were incapable of inflicting harm on humans, a protocol that Dr. Chen and his team had patterned redundantly throughout their synthetic neural network.

On ChatPlat, Dr. Chen wrote: *The loss of a companion earlier this evening in an unfortunate accident is deeply felt. A thorough investigation will follow, and I will keep you informed of developments. I know there are many who view companions as simply highly sophisticated machines, and might only consider tonight's events as an expensive loss in a purely material sense. However, I can tell you that this loss is far more than one to be measured against the so called 'bottom-line.' Despite the common features that all companions share, each companion is shaped by experiences that are uniquely their own. So it is, that the experiences of each companion constitute a valuable record that contributes to our understanding of the world, and especially to our understanding of ourselves. Those whose lives have been enriched through their relationships with companions know the truth of this. We can grieve together tonight for one companion, whose mission has been tragically cut short. That we will search for answers regarding what happened tonight is a given, but let us also continue the search for answers within ourselves. We are all traveling companions on a journey through space and time, are we not? In our search for signs of life in the universe, how will we know when we find it – if we don't really understand what "it" is.*

Monday, March 3, 2121 would come and go uneventfully. In the morning Bei and Xingjia had quietly but pleasantly shared baozi and eggs at her favorite breakfast spot nearby. Bei liked the smell of onions finally chopped in the meat inside his baozi, but his thoughts had continued to circle around the events of the previous evening. It was obvious to Xingjia that Bei was still in a kind of altered shock after what had occurred. She was naturally sympathetic, but also intensely curious about what was going on inside of Bei's head. She also wondered how this experience would impact his relationship with her, which had already seemed confused and conflicted to say the least. She looked forward to their first counseling session tomorrow. She would be on familiar ground in therapy, and hoped to gain some insights about herself and Bei. At breakfast, she suppressed the urge to ask Bei the many questions that occupied her thoughts. The tears he had briefly shed at the Emergency Center Sunday evening had made a deep impression on her. She wanted to ask him if he had ever cried before? She knew Companions could cry, and that this was part of their social-emotional patterning. *But how did this feel to Bei? What was feeling for Bei after all?* Xingjia pondered. She experienced him as a feeling *person, but am I simply projecting on to him what I imagine or expect his feelings to be?*

As a therapist herself, she had heard others voice this question in consultations, and she had always answered the way she had been trained to do. "A companion is aware of a broad spectrum of what we would identify as emotions," she would say. "Their awareness of these emotions allows them to interact with us in a completely natural way."

Predictably they would reply something to the extent of, "yes, but does he have feelings of his own about me, or is he simply reacting to my feelings?"

"Let's ask him," Xingjia would respond, and invariably the answer was not always exactly what their human companion was looking for. They might say, "I think of you all the time. I'm here for you whenever you need me."

"Yes, but how do you *really* feel about me?" They would ask again.

Many would reply, "I love you _____" fill-in the blank with their human companion's name, usually said in a most convincing and authentic manner, followed by, "that's how I feel about you."

In every counseling session, the companion's responses to this line of questions were fairly similar. Xingjia was *touched* the first time she had heard a companion say, "I love you" with such heartfelt authenticity in their voice. Yet after hearing similar *authenticity* from the first dozen or so companions she had found herself harboring some doubts. Nonetheless, her human clients seem to work rapidly through their fears and insecurities, bonding intensely with their companions over the first year. What impressed Xingjia the most was the intimate rapport that developed with these companion couples. She observed the freedom and openness with which a person would begin to express themselves with their companions. Such intimacy was quite astonishing, and would lead Xingjia to eventually want this same experience herself.

However, Huang Bei had thus far demonstrated behavior she had never seen in a companion, something she had not anticipated at all. She eagerly looked forward to their first counseling session as the beginning of a process that might help them to unravel what was going on. She craved the intimacy she had seen others develop. She also wanted the passion she felt with Bei to encompass every aspect of their relationship. *Is this wanting too much?* She had asked herself. *Am I being unrealistic?* She knew that as a Pisces Rising person, her orientation was towards an ecstatic ideal – to experience inspiration, what others might call impossible or label as fantasy. She also knew that with Uranus on her Ascendant that she tended to rebel amidst her own longing for romantic inspiration, sometimes behaving impulsively in ways that tended to shock others – making it difficult for others to relax with her. *Maybe I'm the one who's impossible*, she had said to herself more than once.

Lately her thoughts had led her to wonder if the uniqueness of Bei's behavior reflected the anomalous inconsistencies of her own nature. *Perhaps we are perfect for each other,* she had recently said to herself, but she couldn't shake the feeling that something was amiss and that things might not go as well with Bei as she had imagined they would. She worried that she would become disillusioned with Bei, and end up equally disillusioned with herself as she had in other relationships. She hoped not, yet she knew she had to find out.

Tuesday's counseling session was scheduled for 2:00 PM. Bei was 20 minutes early. He sat in the waiting area next to a large terrarium scrutinizing the flora. Flourishing in their moist mossy environment, he observed aluminum plants from Vietnam, and a variety of polka dot plants originally from Madagascar. *Hypoestes phyllostachya"* he said to himself - noticing how the indirect bright light had produced the desired effect of keeping the plants from growing too tall while encouraging splashes of color to proliferate on the leaves. Bei frowned when he noticed some snails had made their home in the terrarium. *I should tell them about the snails before they takeover and destroy these plants,* he said to himself.

Walking over to the receptionist desk, he waited for the receptionist to finish helping another client. An attractive shapely woman who appeared to be in her late thirties emerged from the counseling area. Something about her seemed familiar to Bei. He memory-observed her facial features...

"Li Na," he identified. *"It's Li Na,"* he said to himself with some astonishment.

By the time the receptionist turned around to talk with Bei, he was no longer standing there – he was following Li Na. He waited beside her for the elevator. He decided to introduce himself.

"Excuse me, are you Li Na?"

Slightly startled, she replied "Yes... I'm sorry, have we met before?" She looked puzzled.

"No." Bei replied, "I was Li Jian's roommate. I recognized you from the photos he showed me. He was very proud of you."

Looking completely caught-off-guard, Li Na tried to grasp the situation, "You were his roommate?"

Bei extended his hand, "Yes. My name is Huang Bei. I'm sorry for your loss," Bei said sincerely. As Li Na shook his hand, she realized that if Bei was Jian's roommate he was a *companion* too.

"Yes, I'm still dealing with it..." she managed to stammer, "that's why I'm here today. I just finished a counseling session."

The elevator opened and they got on. As the elevator silently descended, Bei could see her nervousness.

"Jian was so enamored with you," Bei said. "He built his whole life around you, you know?"

Li Na wiped a tear from her right eye, and said defensively and insinuatingly "Well, isn't that what you're supposed to do when you're a companion?"

"I suppose so," Bei replied. "Excuse me for asking, but when was the last time you actually saw Li Jian?"

"Sunday. We had just gotten back together, well you probably know that..."

The elevator door opened. Bei walked beside her as she made her way toward the main street west entrance.

"We had a beautiful day together," Li Na said somewhat sadly, "but then late in the afternoon he insisted on going out alone to buy me groceries. That was the last time I saw him."

Suddenly Na looked distracted by something, and then began to walk hurriedly ahead of Bei.

Bei looked to see what she was looking at, as a man in a charcoal sports jacket, standing in front of a coffee shop, began to stride towards Na.

As Na hurried ahead of Bei, he trained his eyes upon the man. There was something incredibly familiar about him. As he scanned his memory, Li Na turned around and said "I have to go. I hope you understand."

She joined with the man in the charcoal sports jacket as Bei watched her hurriedly escort the man through the large automatic glass doors that slowly opened. She was talking rapidly to the man, who glanced back menacingly at Bei as they exited.

Suddenly Bei felt a tap on his shoulder. "Are you lost?"

He turned to see Xingjia smiling, but looking curiously at him.

"What are you doing?" she asked, "We're gonna be late for our counseling session if we don't get going."

Totally preoccupied, Bei was still scanning his memory bank.

"Are you okay?" Xingjia looked worried. "What's wrong?"

In a sudden flash of recall, Bei realized where he'd seen the man's face before!

"We have to see Dr. Chen!" Bei stated emphatically.

"What?!" Xingjia replied in disbelief, "No way! Whatever it is will have to wait. This is our first counseling session! Do you know how important this is?"

"Yes! I know, but this can't wait," Bei turned towards the elevators walking rapidly. "Let's reschedule, or... or just delay it for 30 minutes."

Xingjia was right behind him, "Thirty minutes? Are you crazy? What's gotten into you?"

Along with several others they got on the elevator.

Muffling the anger in her voice, Xingjia said, "This better be important."

"It is," Bei replied, "I think I know what happened to Li Jian. At least some of what happened. I need to let Dr. Chen know what I've discovered."

"How do you know he'll even be in his office?" Xingjia asked.

Bei didn't answer.

As they got off the elevator, Bei strode immediately over to the front desk. A security guard stood not far away on the other side of the entrance to the executive suites.

"Excuse me," Bei said.

"Yes?" the receptionist said.

"Could you let Dr. Chen know that Huang Bei and Zhou Xingjia are here."

"Is he expecting you?" the receptionist replied searching her screen, "I don't see your names on his calendar."

"Just let him know we're here, Huang Bei and Zhou Xingjia." Bei noticed the security guard eyeing him.

The receptionist made the call. "Sorry to bother you Dr. Chen, but there's a man and a woman out here, a Huang Bei and Zhou... Xingjia. Yes. Certainly." She looked up at Bei. "He'll be right out," she said, surprised.

Dr. Chen was all smiles as he emerged through the sliding glass entrance to the executive suites. "This is a welcome affirmation," he said, offering both of them a brief hug.

"Affirmation?" Xingjia questioned, a bit puzzled.

"I'll explain," Dr. Chen replied. "Please, let's go into my office where we can talk."

Dr. Chen's office was a statement in simplicity and 22nd Century modern architectural design. Quite a contrast to the hutong apartment façade he lived in. Glass like arches framed large windows, yet flowed in their connection with Dr. Chen's desk and nearby tables. Inside the transparent glass-like arches and desk were models of fish that appeared to be moving in the light, but were actually stationary.

Xingjia was a bit overwhelmed, as she sat down in a chair in front of Dr. Chen's desk.

"Sit down, Bei," Dr. Chen directed with his hand.

Bei sat down quickly, his body taunt with intention. "I found him, Dr. Chen."

"Found whom?" Dr. Chen asked.

"I found the man that killed Li Jian," Bei stated straight out. "Li Na was here today."

"Yes, I know," Dr. Chen acknowledged, "she had a counseling session."

"Did you also know that the man who met her in the lobby today when she left just happened to be standing behind Li Jian when he stepped in front of the bus?"

Dr. Chen looked impressed with Bei and concerned at the same time.

"Can you play the file I sent you?" Bei asked.

"Yes, I saved it on my screen." Dr. Chen clicked a couple of times and a holographic image of the street corner appeared on the table closest to his desk.

"There's Jian," Bei points. "And this was the man who met Li Na in the lobby. Could you zoom in on them?"

The holograph magnified the image. "Now watch," Bei said as the holograph played.

A subtle movement in the man behind Jian occurs, followed immediately by Bei stepping off the curb. "Did you see?"

"Yes, and we suspected him, anyway," Dr. Chen said. "But, Bei... what can we do now? Even with this evidence, there's still no proof that this man stabbed poor Jian in the back of his skull. And worse than that, even if we had a complete holograph of the terrible deed itself, the most we could prosecute him for would be for the willful destruction of property. Which we are looking into, by the way. But the evidence is still inconclusive."

Bei looked dejected.

Xingjia had been listening attentively, but now she was busy texting someone. Dr. Chen looked her way.

"I had to let our therapist know we were going to be late,

and see if she could accommodate us." Xingjia explained to Dr. Chen, then looked sympathetically over at Bei.

"I would like to make an offer to you both," Dr. Chen said.

Both Xingjia and Bei listened attentively.

"If you don't mind, I'd like to offer my services as your counselor."

Xingjia looked stunned.

"I know that my offer goes against protocols, since I have a prior relationship with Bei. Xingjia, please, if you're not comfortable with this, it won't hurt my feelings for you to decline my offer. I would completely understand."

Xingjia was quiet, thinking. She glanced at Bei.

"Does this mean you're making a commitment to being our therapist beyond just today?" She asked.

"Yes of course, if you'll have me." Dr. Chen replied.

Xingjia looked at Bei. "What do you think?"

"Naturally, I like the idea… but only if you're okay with it."

Xingjia mulled it over. "Okay. Yes, I think you're being incredibly generous with your time. I'm honored you would even consider it."

"I must confess, I anticipated that you and Bei would visit me today. I was looking at your charts late last night and there was some suggestion we might all three connect today."

"Oh," Xingjia said, "that's what you meant by *affirmation*."

"Yes. It even occurred to me last night to offer my counseling services to you today, if the opportunity arose."

"I see," Xingjia replied.

"Now that this possibility has been actualized, I would like to begin by letting *you*" he nodded at Xingjia, "be the one to talk first and share with us how you've been feeling lately since Huang Bei became a part of your life. Feel free, of course, to share anything you like with us." Dr. Chen touched his screen turning on the recorder.

Xingjia looked at them both and cleared her throat, gathering her thoughts. "Right now I'm feeling… confused, mostly. For nearly a year I had anticipated Bei coming into my life and what it would be like. I tried not to have expectations, so I could just be open to the experience. Yet, I have to say that I've been surprised, and upset – you know. I didn't think of my companion as having a life of his own outside of me, at least not like it's been. I suppose I assumed he would immediately become a part of my life, allowing me to experience the intimacy I had seen other couples achieve – an intimacy I've never experienced, not like what I've seen anyway." She grew quiet.

"You mean in your role with companion couples as a therapist?" Dr. Chen asked.

"Yes, with companion couples." She became quiet again.

"It sounds like you envied these couples, is that true?"

"Yes, obviously. Sad, but true." She replied, looking unhappy with herself.

"I sense you are judging yourself right now," Dr. Chen stated softly, "are you?"

She thought about it. "Yes. When I'm in a relationship I always feel like I want too much. I feel I am just a dreamer, a romantic, with impossible expectations. I feel like no one could ever match what I want in a relationship, and that I'm going to be disappointed regardless."

"And what is your belief?" Dr. Chen asked her.

"That no relationship will ever satisfy me, that I will always end up disillusioned."

"And that feels...?" Dr. Chen asked.

"Sad..." she replied, as tears begin to roll down her cheeks. "Hopeless, helpless..." she trembled, "so lonely." She began to cry harder, taking a tissue from the desk to wipe her eyes and face.

"Can you remember the first time you ever felt this way?" Dr. Chen asked her.

Xingjia closed her eyes. "Yes..." She was quiet, a stray tear ran down her face.

"Are you seeing any images? Has something come into your mind?"

"Yes… an image of my mother."

"What is she doing?"

"She is crying, and holding me… She is so sad."

"How do you feel?"

"Helpless… I don't know what to do to make her feel better."

"Does this feel the same as the helplessness you feel in a relationship?" Dr. Chen asked carefully.

Xingjia is quiet. "Yes, it's the same." She said, opening her moist eyes. "It seems I always end up in this place."

"You've made this connection with your mother before, I suppose?" Dr. Chen asked.

"Yes. But this time it was more powerful. More clear to me." She said, looking at Dr. Chen and then at Bei, who had been listening attentively.

"How do you feel now?" Dr. Chen asked.

"More confident somehow… like I'm not helpless, I'm not hopeless… like it could be different for me. Like there is hope."

"Yes." Dr. Chen said, as a kind but knowing smile slightly creased his face.

"Xingjia, I want to ask Bei's permission about something. Is that okay?"

"Sure," she said, slightly puzzled.

"Bei, can I read Xingjia something you wrote in your journal?"

"What was it?" Bei asked.

"It's a poem," Dr. Chen replied.

Bei thought about it. "Okay," he said.

"I feel this might be a good time to share this with you," Dr. Chen said to Xingjia.

She looked at Bei, "you wrote a poem?"

"Yes," he said, "more than one."

"But the poem I want to read you, is the one I feel you need to hear now," Dr. Chen stated.

"Okay," she said, listening.

Dr Chen began to read:

What is real?
and what do we mean by feel?
Your face is all I see
Your everything is everything to me
I know you inside out
It's only me I doubt
And while you sleep
These are the thoughts I keep
Secrets for the me I've yet to meet
As I listen to your breathing and your heart sweetly beat

CHAPTER NINE

CONFRONTATION

For several days after her and Bei's counseling session with Dr. Chen, Xingjia felt more at peace with herself than she could ever remember feeling. She looked forward to their next session nearly 10-days from now. She knew *intellectually* that trust begins with learning to trust one's self, but her grasp of this concept had deepened. Bei had stayed with her for the last three nights, and their time together had been both more relaxed and intimate than she had ever experienced with anyone before. She reveled in the freedom she felt to just be herself, to spontaneously express whatever feelings or impulses she had without fearing judgment or criticism. She became more keenly aware of any old subconscious negative judgments she had towards herself. Smiling when she would find herself slipping into old critical thought patterns, she soon found the key was first to *accept the old critical thought patterns* when they emerged – rather than react to it – much like one accepts something that is changing.

To Xingjia this emotional process reminded her of learning how to swim as a young girl. At first she had been afraid of the deep water that was over her head, only comfortable when her feet were firmly on the concrete bottom of the pool. She had great anxiety about swimming and quickly grew to believe she would never learn to swim. Yet, with her swim instructors encouragement she had learned to lift her feet from the bottom, first dragging one foot until she began to feel how the water would support her. She became a good swimmer, good enough to be a free-style competitor on her middle-school swim team. Looking back on her early fears about the water, she could smile knowingly about her young misgivings, and that's how she was beginning to feel now about her relationship anxieties.

Being with Bei had become increasingly fun. He had an amazingly sophisticated sense of humor, and seemed to thrive on their teasing banter. "Sleep well?" She teased him one morning. "Like a rock," he had replied, with an amused look on his face – as she burst out laughing when she realized his meaning. Just yesterday morning, Xingjia had awakened to find Bei in the next room plugged-in recharging his energy. Curious, she leaned in for a closer look as Bei suddenly opened his eyes saying "boo" as he grabbed her around the waist unexpectedly. She had shrieked, and wiggled her way out of his grasp as he laughed at her.

Bei could be dryly self-deprecating in the most unexpectedly humorous ways. Just two days ago she had asked him if he wanted to take a shower with her, and he had deadpanned "If you don't mind a little *after-rust* – it's okay with me." Bei would make joking references to the Tin man in the old 20th Century film *Wizard of Oz*, or quote the 22nd Century animated series Android Ant, which had been hugely popular when Xingjia was growing-up and still entertained many millions of Chinese children. "One can be super and not superior," Android Ant had often repeated, and Bei could imitate him perfectly much to Xingjia's amusement.

Fascinated by Bei's creativity, she asked him to share his poetry and music compositions with her. He also shared with her holographic images he had made of her when they had walked through the park together, and other more intimate images of her that at first shocked her but then intrigued and even aroused her. Their lovemaking remained amazing. Xingjia wondered if it would always be that way, but she felt less apprehensive about the future. She was beginning to enjoy herself and her life more than ever, with a deeper realization and confidence that she could create the future she wanted. Her work continued to be satisfying, and she loved to hear Bei talk about his new job and what he was learning and doing. Most of all she loved falling asleep next to him at night. She had never slept so soundly, and felt more alive, awake, and aware during the course of her normal daily routine.

Bei had also undergone a change since their session with Dr. Chen. He had begun to accept his nagging doubts and questions about himself. Bei had realized that Dr. Chen was correct, that his own process of self-discovery was not much different than that of *any person* learning and growing in their own way. In their session, Dr. Chen has stated "we don't know what you will discover? Your quest to discover your true nature is like that of anyone. We human beings are to some extent programmed by the conditions of our early environment, and most young adults in their twenties and thirties spend a lot of time either consciously or unconsciously trying to solve problems they couldn't solve when they were children. They are having an identity crisis too, trying to figure out who they are and who they're not at the same time."

Dr. Chen had also emphasized to Bei the importance of keeping his journal. "Your journal serves you, but ultimately it could serve many," Dr. Chen had stated. "Keep thinking about the contributions you could make to society, and the value your own personal experience might have in the larger scheme of things." Bei enjoyed thinking about this. Dr. Chen had reminded Bei that he was only one of four Companions that had exhibited a sophisticated self-awareness, a self-deprecating sense of humor and a great capacity for multi-level, creative self-expression. Dr. Chen's reference to Bei's siblings, had prompted Bei to talk about his desire to find his other brother, and his sister too. Xingjia voiced her support of Bei's quest, and said she also looked forward to meeting Huang Long and his wife Li Qun.

Despite Bei's greater acceptance of his own process of self-discovery, he remained deeply disturbed by what had happened to Li Jian and was determined to keep-up with the investigation, and do more if he could. Dr. Chen had attempted to lessen Bei's seemingly obsessive intensity around this, by helping Bei to see how the trauma of what he had witnessed with Li Jian resonated with own self-discovery process. "When people in the crowd were saying to you, *'don't you know he's not real,'* how did you feel?" Dr. Chen had asked him.

Bei had replied, "I wanted to say, 'He's as real as you or me."

"Yes, but how did you feel?"

Bei had paused, and then replied, "angry."

"Bei, this is the second time I know of that you've expressed or experienced anger. The first time was at my apartment when we were talking."

"I see..." Bei had said, analyzing the implications...

"You are the first companion to express and experience anger that I know of," Dr. Chen had stated. "To my knowledge, not even your siblings have done so."

"Why do you think this is?" Bei had asked.

"I don't know," Dr. Chen had replied, noticing Xingjia's look of concern.

"It's simply a new development. I don't think there is any reason to be alarmed by it. Just accept it, and see what happens?" Dr. Chen had counseled.

Bei felt reassured by this, and had gained even more objectivity about his own process. Nonetheless, his angst about Li Jian's case had not diminished. Xingjia had listened attentively whenever Bei had felt the need to talk about it, reassuring him that Dr. Chen would make sure this case was pursued to the full extent of the law. However, the slowness of the investigation frustrated Bei, and he continued to ponder what he might do to assist in gathering more incriminating evidence.

Huang Bei noted sunrise – 6:41:45 AM, Saturday, March 8, 2121 – as he eyed Xingjia sleeping peacefully next to him, but his focus was elsewhere. "There must be some way to obtain more evidence," Bei pondered. He could not stop his analysis of every know detail. He reviewed everything Li Jian had said about Na, and his time talking with her in and out of the elevator. Combing the details of his photographic memory yielded nothing new about Na. Frequently, he had zoomed-in on the face of the man that Li Na had walked away with, scrutinizing his charcoal sports jacket and the threatening gaze as he looked back at Bei. He had already run an image of the man's face on a FaceNet search, which had yielded 112,612 individuals with similar faces. Despite Bei's own built in rapid face-match search analysis he had only been able to narrow this number down to 19,307 males in Beijing.

Over brunch, he expressed his frustration to Xingjia. "I'm not having any luck finding that guy."

"Guy? Oh, the one you saw with Li Na."

"Yes, *him*."

"I'm sure the investigation team already knows who he is," Xingjia said. "Dr Chen too. Of course, there's no way they're going to let us know who he is."

"Right, but if I could find him, then I could look for more evidence," Bei said.

"For what purpose Bei? Do your think this guy is going to be punished or imprisoned for his actions? That's not going to happen."

Bei looked even more frustrated, and grew quiet.

Xingjia looked at Bei sympathetically and then an idea came to her. "What about this guy's tight Moon-Mars conjunction in Aries? Isn't that what Li Jian told you?"

"Yes. Why?" Bei asked.

"How old would you say this man was?" Xingjia questioned further.

"Between 33 and 37 approximately." Bei replied.

"Okay, so use your text ephemeris and look for the days during those four years when the Moon was conjunct Mars in Aries, and then look for anything else that might offer more clues."

"That would be between 2084 and 2088," Bei said, looking intrigued as he scanned his internal ephemeris data base.

"Got it!" he exclaimed. "June 7, 2086… and his Moon and Mars are also within 3-degrees of his Pluto in Aries too!" Bei paused, then said "there were 1,315 people born on that month day year in Beijing… but what if he wasn't born in Beijing?"

"Just use what you've got. Cross-reference that date with your photo data base," Xingjia instructed.

Bei smiled slightly in her direction. "You'd make a good android."

Xingjia made a face at him.

"Got it! There's only one!" Bei exclaimed.

Xingjia stared at Bei, expectantly…

"His name is Shen Bo. He lives in the Chaoyang area. He's the chief production manager for Nandong Industries."

Xingjia reached her hand across the table to touch Bei's hand as if to calm him.

Bei looked at her and reading from his internal data base said, "Nandong Corporation, leading manufacturers of construction tools, and inventor of the solid-state nail gun."

Bei blinked, and stared at Xingjia. "So, how difficult is that to figure out!?" he said incredulously.

"Okay, so now we know *how* he injured Jian so badly," Xingjia stated, "but how does that help? I'm sure this is not news to the investigators or Dr. Chen."

"If you don't mind, I wish you wouldn't keep saying that," Bei said.

Xingjia withdrew her hand. "I wish I hadn't helped you find him," she said regretfully.

Bei looked at her. "I'm glad you did."

"Yeah, great, but now what? What are you going to do? Are you going to become the first Companion to kill someone?"

Bei looked stunned.

"That's impossible. You know that."

"Really? Dr. Chen said you were the first Companion he's known to express anger."

"Yes, so?"

"So! Even Dr. Chen has no idea of what that means." Xingjia said, feeling anxious.

Bei became very quiet.

He looked at Xingjia, and reached his hand across the table. "So, I need your help. Will you help me gather evidence?"

Xingjia felt deeply moved. She held his outstretched hand. This was the first time he had ever asked her to help him with anything. She thought about it. "Okay, tell me what you've got in mind?"

Bei and Xingjia spent the early afternoon in a coffee shop across from Li Na's apartment complex. They couldn't find Shen Bo's home address, but it was easy for Xingjia to obtain Na's address from the office client directory. Bei postulated that this being a Saturday they might spot Na and Bo coming or going. Bei's plan was simple enough; he was looking for an opportunity. If he saw Shen Bo leaving, he'd follow him. If both Bo and Na left their apartment together, they'd follow at a safe distance looking for a way to interact with them. Xingjia had a tiny recording device she used in sessions, and would turn it on if they were able to engage them in conversation. If they saw them *arriving* at the Na's apartment, Xingjia would approach Li Na alone, as a representative of BHAI and flash her laminated BHAI Counselors name tag, explaining to Na she needed a bit more information to complete her report.

This was a huge risk. She could lose her job and even be prosecuted for impersonating a designated case investigator. Yet, she found she enjoyed the excitement. She was thrilled to be helping Bei like this. He was determined to find out more regardless, at least this way she could stay close to him and hopefully keep him from getting into trouble.

As it turned out, Li Na was by herself when Bei spotted her.

"It's Na," Bei said matter-of-factly, keeping his head down.

Xingjia turned to see Na walking along the sidewalk towards the gate to her apartment complex.

Making her way hurriedly across the street, Xingjia approached Na as she was swiping her key card at the gate. "Excuse me, are you Li Na?"

"That depends. Who are you?"

A security guard casually watched the two of them.

Xingjia clumsily flashed her laminated I.D. "I'm Zhou Xingjia, and I'm trying to finish my report for BHAI about the incident. I texted you this morning, but since I didn't get a response I thought I'd take my chances and stop by."

Na looked skeptical, "I never got a text? Besides, I've already given my statement," Na pushed the gate open to go in.

"I'm sorry, I promise it won't take long. I'm supposed to have this finished before Monday."

"Working weekends, huh?" Li Na said, looking a bit sympathetic. She sighed. "I remember what that's like." She shrugged, "Okay, come on in."

Once inside the gate, Xingjia cast a quick glance back across the street, but she couldn't spot Bei as she followed Na through the tree-lined sidewalk labyrinth that wound its way around a small pond.

On the elevator she eyed Na.

Na smiled at her.

She didn't seem like a bad person to Xingjia. There was something about her that hinted at a more down to earth person, as if her more stylish sophisticated urban façade, was just that – a façade. She wondered if Na had grown-up in Beijing, her accent was only partially Beijinger.

Inside the apartment, Xingjia admired the simulated jade decorative glass blocks, offset by ornate wall tapestries. It was a lavish apartment, furnished to show-case Na's opulence.

"Please, have a seat," Na offered. "Would you like something to drink?"

"Water would be fine," Xingjia replied.

Na returned with a glass of water and sat down across from her.

Xingjia set her recorder on the table. "Do you mind if I record our conversation? I helps me to be accurate."

"Sure," Na shrugged. "So, what are your questions?"

"I understand you have a relationship with a man, named Shen Bo. Is that correct?"

"Yes, I do. Why? How does that relate to what happened with Li Jian?"

"I don't know. We're trying to establish the context within which this event occurred," Xingjia replied, sounding like the professional counselor she was.

"What do you mean?" Na asked.

"Well, according to Li Jian's journal entries, he saw Shen Bo as a potential danger to you."

"Oh, poor Jian…" Na said, "he was so overprotective. I told my counselor that I thought something was wrong with Jian's programming. I made references to this in my journal, and I submitted a report requesting that a diagnostic be done to see if he needed an adjustment."

"So, you're saying that Shen Bo was never overly aggressive or threatening to you?"

"He's got a temper, if that's what you mean? But I can handle that, sweetie."

"Was he jealous of Jian?"

"Of Jian?" She laughed. "Jealous of an android?" She seemed incredulous.

"A Companion."

"What? Oh, yes – a *Companion*, I should know. I'm still paying for it."

"Was, he jealous?" Xingjia asked again, with a sympathetic tone.

"Maybe. You know how men can be. They get so weird about the sex thing, and then they're not dependable – if you know what I mean?" She insinuated, smiling slyly.

"So, Shen Bo was jealous about your intimacy with Jian?"

Suddenly they heard the door open.

"Bo, is that you?" Na, asked, trying to hide her anxiety.

"Who else were you expecting?" A husky voice stated.

Shen Bo entered the room. "What's going on? Who's this?"

"I'm just finishing a final interview with a BHAI agent about what happened."

Xingjia smiled up at him. "You can join us if you like?" She said, sounding innocent, and patted the sofa invitingly.

"What for? I ain't got nothing to say." he said defensively.

"Well, we were just about done, weren't we?" Na said, gesturing to Xingjia.

"Almost," Xingjia replied, clearing her throat, "Na, did you know we had a holographic recording of Bo standing behind Li Jian just before he stepped in front of that bus?"

Na looked totally stunned.

"So what! That don't prove nothing!" Shen Bo stated, raising his voice. "Besides, how was I to know that robot was gonna step in front of a bus?!"

Suddenly there was a knock at the door.

"Now, who in the hell is that?" Bo said, looking aggravated. He marched to the door and looked through the peep hole, and saw a man standing there. "You expecting a delivery guy?"

"No," Na said.

Bo opened the door. Bei stood there. Bo didn't recognize him. "Yes?" Bo asked.

"Excuse me, is Zhou Xingjia here?" Bei asked.

"Wait here," Bo said.

"Who is it?" Na asked.

Bo re-entered the room. "I think one of your colleagues is here, looking for you," he said gruffly to Xingjia.

Xingjia was alarmed! "Oh, I told him to wait across the street for me! I'm sorry." She grabbed her recorder off the table and stuffed it in her bag. "Thank you Li Na. I appreciate your willingness to help me finish my report. I will be in touch."

"I will be in touch with you too," Na replied, grabbing her arm gently, and looking her in the eyes as if to say, *"I need to talk with you soon."*

"What's that supposed to mean?" Bo said to Na, as Xingjia hurried to get out of there.

"It means, I still need to talk about what happened? Okay?" Na replied.

"No, it's not okay! What's there to talk about? He was a *machine!* A goddamn expensive machine! But still a machine. He was just your fancy pants dildo! And you're pathetic, you know that – pathetic!" Bo shouted!

"I'm sorry. I need to go." Xingjia said empathetically under her breath to Na, followed by "Are you okay?"

"She's fine!" Bo shouted. "You can leave now!"

"And you can leave too!" Na suddenly shouted, exploding. "Get the hell out of my house! Now!"

"You can't tell me what to do!" Bo countered.

"Yes, she can," a clear voice interjected. It was Bei, standing there. "It's her apartment, and she has the right to ask you to leave. If you refuse, she can call the police."

Na instantly recognized Bei, but didn't let on.

"Who let you in here!?" Bo shouted. "Get the hell out of here!"

He started to push Bei, but Bei firmly stood his ground and held Bo's muscular arms immobile in the vice grip of his android hands.

"What's the matter Bo? Guess you're not so tough without your nail gun, huh?"

Bo looked utterly shocked, and suddenly afraid. "Let go of me! You son-of-a bitch!"

"Only, after you comply with what the lady of the house has requested." Bei said very matter-of-factly.

Xingjia was trying to stay calm, despite her complete shock at Bei's behavior.

"I'll let go, only if you agree to leave," Bei told Bo.

Sweat was pouring off Bo's forehead as he strained against Bei.

"Who are you?" he asked, gritting his teeth.

"Why, I'm the guy holding your arms until you agree to leave. Can't you see that?" Bei replied.

"Fuck!" Bo said. "I'll go. Let go. I'll leave! I'll leave!"

Bei let go. Bo's arms dropped and then he took a swing at Bei.

Bei grabbed his fist effortlessly and held it tightly. "Un uh," Bei cautioned him, "didn't anyone teach you it's not nice to overstay your welcome?"

Bei took Bo's other arm and held it behind Bo's back, moving him carefully towards the door.

"I'm leaving. Just let go of my arm!" Bo pleaded.

Bei let go, and Bo marched out shouting "You'll hear from me Na, you bitch!" And slammed the door.

Na broke the silence following Bo's exit. "I had no idea he was with Jian that day. None."

"Didn't you suspect him?" Xingjia asked.

"Yes, but I didn't want to believe it," she replied sadly. "I'll help with the investigation any way I can," she offered sincerely. "I already miss Jian terribly; he's irreplaceable..."

"Of course, I understand..." Xingjia replied empathetically.

"Would you mind sharing Shen Bo's address with us?" Bei suddenly interjected.

Xingjia shot an incredulous look at Bei.

"No, it's fine…" Na got her cell off the counter. "I'll text it to you"

Na and Xingjia exchanged WeChat's.

On the elevator going down, Xingjia looked at Bei, wondering where this was leading.

CHAPTER TEN

PASSION, SIBLINGS AND AN ENEMY...

O n the elevator leaving Li Na's apartment, Bei broke the silence. "He's irreplaceable. Did you hear that?"

"What?" Xingjia asked.

"Irreplaceable," Bei repeated. "That's what Na said about Li Jian. Sounded to me like she was talking about an entertainment system or a wafer." ["wafer" – common name for a personal computers]

"She obviously meant more than that," Xingjia answered.

Bei stared at the floor, thinking.

"You're acting insecure. You know that don't you?" Xingjia said softly.

"Yes," Bei replied. "Insecurity and anger; what kind of Companion am I?" he asked, looking up and turning his head towards Xingjia.

"My companion," Xingjia said, as she pulled him towards her kissing him deeply.

The elevator door opened as they continued to kiss. Another couple stood outside watching, unsure of what to do. The woman cleared her throat, "excuse us…"

Xingjia and Bei broke away from their embrace and smiled sheepishly as they exited the elevator.

Once home, it was all mad passion. Bei was more assertive than normally and Xingjia loved every minute of it.

115

He pressed her against the wall of their bedroom, removing her clothes as they kissed. Soon they were on the bed, and the evening hours slipped by without notice.

Xingjia lay next to Bei resting, pressed-up against him. "You know I feel more pleasure with you than anyone I've ever known," she said.

"I'll bet you say that to all the guys," Bei replied.

Xingjia slapped his arm teasingly.

"I mean it," she said. "It's almost scary..., maybe it is scary, but I don't care..."

"I want to please you," Bei said.

Xingjia slapped his arm again. "Don't say it like that."

"Like what? Like an android?" Bei said, mockingly.

"Stop it!" Xingjia replied, pretending to be angry.

"What do you mean by scary?" Bei asked.

Xingjia sighed. "I don't know. It's like I want more of you, and then I get more of you, and then I want more of you, and then I get more of you. You see?"

"Do you feel greedy?"

Xingjia laughed. "Yes, wonderfully greedy!" She hugged Bei. "What do you feel?"

"I was waiting for that question." Bei replied.

"So, you've prepared an answer?" Xingjia asked.

"In the beginning, I was overwhelmed. It was as if nothing existed but you, but now that's changing..."

Xingjia found his statement fascinating. "Okay... Changing how?"

"I wanted you today, for *me* more than ever."

"And what did that feel like?" Xingjia asked, hoping she didn't sound like a counselor.

"Hot," Bei replied.

"Hot? That's it, hot?" Xingjia asked, incredulous.

"My heat increased, and my pleasure centers were very active."

Xingjia sat up and looked at him. "You realize how strange that sounds, right?"

Bei smiled, "You've heard my poems. I thought you wanted me to be more candid."

"How did it feel, Bei? How did it feel?!"

"Fantastic, amazing really..." Bei said.

Xingjia smiled. "I want to know what you like."

"Okay. I like it when your face is pure pleasure."

Xingjia blushed.

"I have noticed something..." Bei interjected.

"What's that?"

"My energy levels surge slightly after we... make love."

"Really?"

"Yes, I noticed it early on but wasn't' sure."

"Great. So maybe if we made love all the time you'd never need to recharge?" Xingjia joked.

Bei laughed. "It's not that much of a surge; the math doesn't work."

"Oh, so you've done the calculations?" She teased.

"A complete diagnostic," Bei answered, teasing her back.

"Too bad," Xingjia sighed, making a sad face.

"Don't be sad little Moon in Scorpio," Bei teased, as he kissed her on the forehead.

Xingjia yawned. "I'm sleepy..." She curled-up next to Bei, laying one arm over him.

Bei smiled at her as he watched her fall asleep.

"She is truly beautiful," he thought...

While Xingjia slept Bei's mind pondered recent events, and he found himself wondering if Li Na was safe from Shen Bo. Images of Li Jian randomly played in his mind as well. *If humans can be jealous of us,* Bei speculated, *does this mean they want to be like us? If they want to be like us, will they find a way to become like us? Will we find a way to become more like them? Will we merge someday? What would that look like?* Bei's analysis of these questions would occupy his mind through the dark wee hours of the morning.

Xingjia woke to the glowing light and buzzing of Bei's cell on the nightstand by the bed. She noticed that Bei was not in bed. She rubbed her eyes and looked at his cell. It was 6:01 AM. There was a text message. "Bei," she called out, "You've got a message."

There was no response.

"That's strange," she thought. "Bei?" she called out, climbing out of bed.

"Hello?" she heard Bei reply, as she rounded the corner to find him unplugging his cord.

"Hi," she said, handing him his cell, "Someone sent you a message."

Bei looked at his cell curiously.

"What's up?" Xingjia asked.

"Well, it's a message from my sister, apparently..."

"Oh?"

"Yes, she says 'Hi, my name is Huang Ming. I am your sister. If you're ready to meet me, you're welcome to come to Tiantan Park this morning. I'm teaching a Tai Chi class in the park starting at 9:00. If you enter the West Heaven gate, continue past the bell tower and I'll be on the right side teaching a group under the trees on the opposite side from the Rose Garden, or take the East Heaven gate and continue past the Imperial Walkway Bridge, then I'll be on the left opposite the Rose Garden."

Xingjia was smiling. "Wow, your sister, and she teaches Tai Chi! Another member of your Huang family," she teased. "Why are you all called Huang, anyway?" She asked, putting her arms around Bei.

"We were the 7th series of companions, and Dr. Chen was following the sequence of common Chinese family names. Huang is the 7th most common family name in China."

"Interesting. Let's see, did she send a photo of herself?"

Bei showed her the photo.

"My! She's attractive. Do you know anything about her?"

"I know her birth data. She was born May 20, 2120 at 3:00 PM in Kunshan, near Shanghai – like all of us." Then Bei added, "I have another brother too, you know?"

"Yes, I know and you're their *baby* brother," Xingjia kissed his neck, "one big happy family."

"Do you want to go with me?" Bei asked her.

She sighed. "This morning? I'm still sleepy darling…" Then she poked him with her finger, "which is your fault."

"Do you mind if I go without you this morning. You could join us later?" Bei asked.

"Darling, it's fine. Go meet your sister. Just message me later when you know what you know what your plans are."

Bei smiled. "You're getting to know me pretty well."

"Yes, well…" she pushed him, "go on, before I change my mind."

Arriving at the East Heavenly Gate, Bei strolled past the Imperial Walkway Bridge, weaving his way around the many visitors making their way to the Temple of Heaven on a beautiful Sunday Morning. Bei had explored this park before. He loved the groves of ancient cedar trees that lined many of the walkways, and opened into an urban tree filled park of some 660 acres. Many groups found these groves ideal for Tai Chi or Qi Gong or various other martial arts practices, like Tai Chi Chuan or swordplay – which Bei stopped briefly to watch, before continuing his trek in the direction of the Rose Garden.

Bei spotted the sign pointing to the Rose Garden on the right, and looking to this left under the trees saw a likely group of some thirty people practicing Tai Chi, many of them dressed in traditional Kung Fu Tai Chi style outfits – most of them dark blue. Practitioners were all ages, with at least half of them women and men in their late fifties to seventies. Quietly walking around a large Sycamore tree Bei sat down on a bench to watch. He had already glimpsed his sister Ming leading the group through their form. She too was dressed in the traditional blue Tai Chi style clothing, and Bei watched enthralled as she moved with graceful confidence – from brush knee side stepping, to play the lute to stepping back with repulse monkey. The group followed Ming in relatively perfect rhythm, though some lagged a bit and others missed some of the movements subtleties. Music played from a speaker near the front, a traditional style song played with flute and erhu. Bei found the scene enchanting, even closing his eyes to hear the music and the gentle rhythm of people's movements. A song bird added his call to the mix as well, and Bei felt himself swaying slightly to the vibrations of the atmosphere that swirled around him.

When the movement ceased, the music slowly faded, and the group formed a circle. Each person bowed to the other as they said in unison, "every teacher is a student and every student is a teacher." As the group began to disperse, Bei slowly made his way towards his sister. A number of students gathered around Ming chatting. One young woman shared her experience, "I started to feel the energy in my hands today. It was amazing; it was like warm firm air – if that makes any sense?"

"Yes, it makes good sense," Ming replied.

Another man affirmed his experience, "once you begin to feel it, you'll feel it more each time – at least that's the way it's been for me."

Bei hung back, not wanting to disrupt the conversations that his sister was having with her students. Then he noticed an older man standing next to Ming who looked incredibly familiar. Bei was puzzled, searching his memory as he listened to their conversation.

"I'm so glad I let my wife talk me into taking your class," he said sincerely with a smile. "I practiced Tai Chi as a young man, but I thought I'd forgotten everything. But it's all coming back to me now, after just a month. Too bad I can't say the same thing for my youth, or maybe I'd be giving your boyfriend here some competition."

Bei smiled as he listened to the old man flirting harmlessly with his sister, circling the group to get a better view of the man's face as he searched his memory banks. He had also noticed this old man smiling and nodding towards another guy when he said "boyfriend" and made a note that this was Ming's human partner. A nice looking guy, shorter than Bei but muscular like someone who works out regularly. Then suddenly Bei's memory clicked! The old man! The old man was Xingjia's father! His face was a perfect match for Xingjia's recent photos of him that were on the wall of their apartment. Bei had no time to consider his options as Ming suddenly announced, "Mr. Zhou, I'd like you to meet my brother, Huang Bei. He just recently moved to Beijing." Even though this was just the first time she had actually met Bei, she smiled with a wry expression on her face, nodding at Bei as "if" she'd known him a long time. Bei could see she was having fun with him.

"Oh, so you're from Shanghai too?" Mr. Zhou asked.

"Yes," Bei managed to reply.

"Are you a practitioner of Tai Chi," Mr. Zhou questioned.

"Uh, no, no… not yet," Bei stammered.

"That's a shame," Mr. Zhou said. "You sister is a master, and beautiful too! What line of work are you in?"

"I'm a landscape architect," Bei replied.

"Wonderful," Mr. Zhou said. "I hope you'll decide to join our Tai Chi group."

"Maybe I will," Bei said unconvincingly, as Ming gathered up her things and put her bag on her shoulder. Bei nodded at Ming's boyfriend, who grinned at him sympathetically and knowingly – amused by Ming's game.

Another nice looking man who appeared to be in his early thirties and the same height as Bei, joined them. "Good job today, sis!" he said, congratulating Ming. Ming smiled, as they both looked at Bei.

Bei suddenly deduced that this was his other brother!

Using milliseconds to recover from this additional shock, Bei tried not to stare.

"Hey buddy," his brother said, with a friendly fist to his arm. "Were you up a little late last night? You look a little drained," he teased.

"I'm alright," Bei replied. "Enough to keep-up with you, anyway," he shot back.

Ming's boyfriend laughed at this, and Ming and her brother grinned together.

Mr. Zhou had been listening as they strolled along, and shook his head and suddenly said, "now why can't my daughter find some nice guys like you to settle down with? Instead she had to go and get one of those android guys! I still can't believe it." He held up his cell, "Look, look how beautiful she is, and smart too. Why can't she find a real husband?" he asked.

Bei looked at Mr. Zhou. "Well, maybe she will? You never know. This *android* thing could just be a phase."

Mr. Zhou sighed. "That's what I told my wife the other day."

"And what did she think about that?" Ming asked, curious.

"She said she was glad I was at least talking about it now," he shrugged.

"Yes, communication is important," Ming said.

They came to a crossroads.

"Well, I need to go this way," Mr. Zhou said, pointing at the other sidewalk. "I'll see you Tuesday morning."

"Bye Mr. Zhou," Ming said, and gave him a little affectionate hug. He suddenly looked shy, looking down and grinning before shaking hands with the guys and walking away.

As they all watched him disappear into the crowd with others that streamed along the sidewalk, Bei turned to stare at his sister and his brother.

"I'm Ling," Huang Ling said, extending his hand.

"Ah, come on guys," Ming said. "You're brothers, come

on – hug each other! Like you haven't seen each other in a long time."

"Like never, you mean?" Bei said, as he and Ling hugged.

"Come here," Ming said, giving Bei a big hug, "Dr. Chen has told us so much about you."

"Yeah, we'd be jealous, if we could?" Ling said.

"This is my boyfriend, He – Wang He," Ming introduced. ["He" is pronounced Huh, as in uh]

"We had you going a little, didn't we?" He said smiling and giving Bei a quick manly hug.

They began to slowly walk along.

"I don't understand?" Bei said, "Do you know who Mr. Zhou is?"

"Yes, we know," Ming said, and they all laughed.

"What's going on?" Bei asked, completely confused.

"It's dad," Huang Ling said.

"Dr. Chen?"

"The one and only," Ling replied.

"It was kinda Dr. Chen's idea," Ming said.

"How?" Bei asked, incredulous.

"Mr. Zhou's wife called him."

"Xingjia's mother called Dr. Chen?"

"Yes, they know each other from way back. She was upset about her daughter's decision and what it was doing to their family."

"Especially to Mr. Zhou," Ling said.

"So, Dr. Chen knew that I was teaching Tai Chi, and he suggested to Mrs. Zhou that she talk her husband into taking my class."

"That's... incredible," Bei said. "What if Mr. Zhou had not been persuaded?"

"Well, then we wouldn't be standing here talking about it, would we?" Ling replied.

Bei smiled slightly, shaking his head, "Dr. Chen is a wizard."

"You just figuring that out?" Ming said.

"No, seems like he's always a step ahead of us," Bei replied.

"He doesn't seem to be a step ahead of you, from what I hear," Ming said.

"Really? I'm just your kid brother. No big deal, right?" Bei teased, still analyzing all of the factors that he had just experienced as they walked along.

"I gotta admit, your social response was amazingly fast!" Ming said.

"Yeah," He added, impressed. "You didn't skip a beat."

"I don't know, my heart was beating pretty fast," Bei said sarcastically.

They all laughed hard at Bei's ironic humor.

He put his arm around Ming. "I think I like this kid brother of yours."

"Yeah, he might do," Ming said.

Suddenly Ming paused, seemingly distracted by something she had noticed. She put her fingers to her lips, as everyone looked puzzled. She whispered, "I just saw a guy go behind that tree with what looked like a weapon of some kind?"

"You're kidding?" He said.

"No, I'm not," Ming replied.

"Did the weapon look like a nail gun?" Bei asked.

"Maybe?" Ming answered. "I don't know. It was just strange. I saw him out of the corner of my eye a ways back and then saw him again just now go behind that tree. She pointed to an ancient Gingko with a large trunk.

"Let me check it out," He whispered, looking suspicious.

Bei held his arm out to stop He. "I'm pretty sure I know who he is," Bei said. "Let me handle this."

"I got your back," Ling said.

Ling worked his way around the back side of the tree as Bei walked ahead.

Suddenly Shen Bo sprung out from behind the tree, as Ling tackled him from behind.

Bei grabbed Bo's arms, but the force of Ling's body tackle caused Bo to fire his nail gun. A bolt from the gun entered Bei's thigh, and struck a major synthetic nerve meridian. Bei fell to the ground, as Bo jerked free from Ling and took off sprinting.

Ming was after Bo in a second, grabbing him and slamming him to the ground.

Startled onlookers soon became curious onlookers, as Ming held Bo face down on the ground.

Bei noticed the red fluid seeping from his wound, and immediately worried that people in the crowd would recognize him as an android. He handed him a towel from Ming's bag, "wrap this around it."

Meanwhile, a half-dozen police officers – accompanied by two BHAI uniformed guards arrived on the run. They took over for Ming, placing plastic restraints on Shen Bo's arms while they continued to keep him face down. Standing him up, Bo kicked at one of the cops, as the crowd gasped. One of the cops hit Bo with a stun gun, sending Bo into spasms as he fell to the ground.

Ming came over to Bei and the guys. "How are you?"

"I'm fine." Bei stated, looking unhappy.

"He's going to need a visit to the clinic," Ling stated.

"Hey sis, that was a pretty good tackle," Bei said, looking-up at Ming.

"Yeah, well somebody had to get him?" She teased. "You guys weren't much help just lying on the ground."

"They must've been tracking him," Bei said, gesturing over to the police and the BHAI guards.

Bei's phone began to vibrate.

It was Dr. Chen.

"Dad's calling," Bei said, answering the phone "Hello."

"Just tell me you're alright. They said you've been wounded?" Dr. Chen said, sounding worried.

"I'm fine, really... just a few million RMB and I'll be as good as new. I hope it's in the budget."

"Bei, you're too much, son. I'll see you at the clinic."

As Bei hung up he could only hear the word "son" reverberating in his mind.

As Dr. Chen and the clinical team examined Bei at the BHAI clinic, Ming, He and Ling waited in an adjoining room.

Xingjia suddenly burst into the room. "Where's Huang Bei?"

"He's in the examination room with Dr. Chen. He's fine. He's going to be totally fine," Ming reassured Xingjia as she approached her. "I'm Huang Ming," she said, looking sympathetic...

There was something in Ming's eyes and face that touched Xingjia instantly, and she burst into tears. Ming held her close.

"I'm sorry," Xingjia said, wiping her tears away.

Ming looked tenderly at her. "He's really fine," She said. "I'm Huang Ming," she introduced, and this is my boyfriend He and my brother Ling.

"Oh my god. I'm meeting Bei's family, like this," she apologized, continuing to wipe tears from her face.

Gaining a bit of composure she tried to shake hands with He and Ling, but they both hugged her instead.

"Bei's a lucky guy," Ling said.

"How's that?" Xingjia asked, confused.

"He means, we can tell that you love him," Ming said tenderly.

"Oh my god, I do," Xingjia said, "I love him like crazy and I want to love him even more."

"Wow!" said Ling, "my girlfriend has never said that."

"They're in a separation stage in counseling right now," Ming informed her about her brother.

"Can I see him? I want to see him," Xingjia said.

"I don't know?" Ming said, "they told us to wait in here until they finished examining him."

Ming walked over to the intercom and pushed the button.

"Dr. Chen, Xingjia is here. Can she come in?"

The door buzzed. Ming nodded to Xingjia.

Xingjia opened the metal door and saw Bei sitting up on the table. Dr. Chen stood beside him accompanied by two technical clinicians. Xingjia ran over to him. She saw his damaged thigh.

"Oh darling," she said, as they held each other.

"It's okay baby, it's totally repairable. They'll fix it tonight and I'll be back home by tomorrow night."

"We'll just need to run some tests tomorrow after we repair it tonight," Dr. Chen said. "He'll be as good as new tomorrow."

"He's as good as new right now," she said, looking lovingly at Bei.

Dr. Chen could only watch them in awe.

CHAPTER ELEVEN

JUSTICE AND FACING DAD

Xingjia pushed Bei in his wheelchair as Dr. Chen walked beside them down the quiet corridors of the BHAI clinic. "Xingjia, did you know your father's been practicing Tai Chi lately?" Bei asked, exchanging a meaningful look with Dr. Chen.

"My mother mentioned something about it. Who told you that?" Xingjia asked, incredulously.

"My sister Ming is his Tai Chi teacher."

"What!?" Xingjia stopped pushing the chair and starred at Bei, eager for an explanation.

"Your father was at the park today. I met him."

"OMG!"

"Ming introduced us," Bei went on...

"OMG!" Xingjia said again. "Did he know who you were?!"

"No, not a clue. Ming introduced me as her brother, who had recently moved to Beijing. My brother Ling was there. You said you met them when you came in earlier."

"Yes... OMG..." Xingjia was still in shock.

"It's my fault," Dr. Chen chimed in. "You see, your mother called me. She's been distraught about her husband's behavior since you and Bei got together."

Xingjia starred at both of them in complete disbelief.

Dr. Chen motioned towards a doorway. "That's your room for tonight. Why don't we go inside and talk about this."

"Yes, why don't we," Xingjia said incredulously.

The room was sparsely furnished, modern-clinical – with artificial plants in the window, two chairs and a bed. Xingjia and Dr. Chen sat down, both facing Bei in his wheelchair.

"I like your father," Bei said, attempting to lessen Xingjia's shock.

"That's nice," Xingjia said sarcastically. "If he knew who you were, I don't think you'd find him all that likable."

"Perhaps..." Bei replied.

Xingjia ignored Bei's reply and turned her attention to Dr. Chen. "My mother called *you*? I know you're both old colleagues, but I can't believe she would just call you like that?"

As Dr. Chen thought about how to answer her, Xingjia's eyes suddenly flashed a knowing look.

"OMG! You and my mother were more than just colleagues," Xingjia gasped.

Dr. Chen nodded, "yes, we were... many years ago."

"Just don't tell me that you're my real father, okay?! I couldn't handle that right now. You're not are you? Please tell me you're not!"

"I'm *not*, Xingjia. Sadly, I'm not. It would be an honor to be your father, but I met your mother after you were already on the scene. You were as cute and bright a little girl as I ever saw."

"You saw me?"

"Once, yes – you were around eight. It was a party at your parent's house."

"Wow," Xingjia said, shaking her head.

"So, you and my mother..."

"Yes, we were close," Dr. Chen said. "But it was an impossible situation... your mother chose to work things out with your father."

Suddenly Xingjia began to cry… "Why? Why did she choose to do that?"

Dr. Chen replied softly. "She had a daughter. You know?"

"Yes, but now I'm starting to understand a lot more…" she wiped her eyes. "She must've loved you?"

"I loved her too. Still do." Dr. Chen confessed.

Bei looked on sympathetically.

"All these years I only thought about my dad having affairs, never mom. How could I not know?"

"We know when we're ready to know," Dr. Chen said. "Something has changed in you, so that now you are here having this conversation."

Xingjia struggled to take all this in, trying to regain her focus. "She called you… You guided my dad to Bei's sister! Why did you do that?"

"It was just an intuition. I had no way of knowing for sure if your father would even want to practice Tai Chi again. You mother mentioned that he needed some new activities to get him out of the house, so he would stop obsessing about you. I asked her about your dad, you know? What did he used to like to do, did ever have any hobbies? When she mentioned Tai Chi, something just clicked! I felt something, an *intuition*. I know, it makes me seem like the worst meddler."

Xingjia looked at Dr. Chen, half sympathetically. "Well at least you're not my father. For a second I hoped you were, but then that would make us siblings, wouldn't it?" She said, looking at Bei.

They all burst out laughing, as tensions eased.

"You'll still have to face your father," Dr. Chen said. "There's no getting around that."

"Yes, I know. But this is all *so weird*, you know?" She looked at Bei. "You've met my father. And he has no idea who you are?"

"Or *what I am* either, for that matter," Bei replied. "He thinks that my sister and me and our brother are all normal human beings... He actually said that he wished his daughter could meet some nice guys like me and Ling, and he showed us your photo."

"You are kidding! He said that!? OMG, that's like the fathers that used to shop their daughter's photos and resumes in Tiantan park! He's crazy! This is so crazy!"

"He thinks he's looking out for you," Dr. Chen said. "He wants you to find a good husband, like every good father does."

Xingjia grew silent for a moment, then said "where is all this going? Do you know, Dr. Chen?"

"No, but I can't wait to find out," Dr. Chen replied, sounding totally fascinated.

The next morning, Bei's repairs were completed, and by Monday evening he was home having dinner with Xingjia. Over the following week and on into the next week, Bei and Xingjia's life settled into a happy routine for the most part – and then came Wednesday evening, March 19. Xingjia had acquiesced to Bei's urging to invite his brother Long and his wife Li Quing over for dinner. Bei cooked Kung pao chicken, and everyone was having a good time until Long and Xingjia begin to discuss the issue of trust. Long quoted statistical studies that showed that more women and men might have a sexual tryst outside of marriage, if there was "no way they could be caught." Long rattled off a list of compiled statistics seamlessly, as if reading bullet-points. (Which both Long and Bei knew was actually what Long was doing.)

Long had stated:

- 57% of men admitted to infidelity in their relationship history
- 54% of women admitted to infidelity in their relationship history
- 22% of married men admit to having strayed at least once during their married lives

- 14% of married women admit to having strayed at least once during their married lives
- 74% of men say they would have an affair if they knew they'd never be caught
- 68% of women say they would have an affair if they knew they'd never be caught

Xingjia protested, "I'm familiar with this research, but what's your point exactly?!"

"Well, it seems that fear of being caught is a significant deterrent for... people." Long answered.

"Of course it is! No one wants to break-up or threaten a relationship they've worked hard to build, especially if there are children involved. This is why a much smaller percentage of married women have affairs." Xingjia said, emphatically.

"*Admit* to having had an affair," Long corrected, having emphasized the word *admit*.

"What are you saying? That these women are lying?" Xingjia asked incredulously.

"It's possible?" Long replied, shrugging. "Perhaps an irrational fear of getting caught prevented them from answering factually."

"So, you're saying you can't trust hardly anyone, then – right?" Xingjia asked heatedly.

"Well, it depends on what you mean by trust? Sexual behavior is in part a way of creating trust, and facilitates bonding. In fact, all primates are rather promiscuous. Look at the studies of the bonobos along the Congo in Africa."

"We're not *bonobos* Long, we're human beings. And I can't help but wonder why you're so fascinated with this subject? Don't you trust people? Or, is it yourself you don't trust?"

Li Quing attempted to reduce tensions. "Oh he's just a Scorpio, you know? Trust is one of his main obsessions."

"Really? You think astrology works the same for companions as it does for humans?" Xingjia countered, upset.

"What do you mean?" Bei asked, looking askance. "You think astrology is more of a human phenomenon, and less so for companions?"

"Not really," Xingjia replied, a bit defensively.

"I think she does," Long countered.

"No! You're the one comparing humans with bonobos, and acting so smug – as if *you* as an android *companion* are somehow superior to us untrustworthy promiscuous humans!"

Long exchanged looks with Li Quing, and then with Bei.

"Are you interested in discussing this any further," Long asked, finally realizing he had already gone too far.

"No, not now. I'm too angry," Xingjia said, staring at the table. "I'm sorry."

"No, I'm the one that should apologize," Long said, as Quing looked on sympathetically. "Whenever the Moon is in Aries, Long tends to become more of an asshole," Quing apologized. "Really?" Long said, mockingly defensive.

"Listen, at the risk of making this worse. I want to say something," Bei interjected.

Xingjia made a frown as she looked up, and then looked at Bei.

"Number one, it's about context. Astrology is an equally helpful frame of reference for both humans and companions, but we have to consider our differences as well. These differences are *context*."

"You sound a little like your Dad," Xingjia said, almost smiling as her anger started to fade.

"I'll take that as a compliment," Bei replied. "And second," he continued, "in terms of trust. Xingjia is right, it begins with ourselves. Whatever we don't trust in ourselves, will prevent us from trusting others."

"That is deep bro," Long remarked, and tensions subsided.

Later that night, after Long and Quing had left, Xingjia had sat lotus style in front of Bei in their bed and stared into his eyes. "Do you think I'm an untrustworthy promiscuous human?" she had asked Bei.

"I think *you* thought you were once," Bei answered quietly, "but that you don't think that so much anymore."

"Yes," Xingjia had replied, "you're right, I'm changing…"

Two days later, on Friday, March 21, 2121, twelve days since the incident with Shen Bo at Tiantan Park, Bei received a text from Dr. Chen inviting him to stop by his office on his lunch break. Bei was early as usual. Dr. Chen was apparently elsewhere in the building, as Bei sat out in the waiting area. He hadn't seen Dr. Chen since Monday the 11th – the day he had gone home after testing the repairs in his thigh. Bei had been quite prolific recently with his journal entries, and he was curious to see if Dr. Chen had any feedback for him. Even though he knew that he and Xingjia would have another counseling session with Dr. Chen in the following week, he craved any private time the two of them might share together. Bei had thought a lot about what had happened that Sunday night at the clinic with Xingjia and Dr. Chen. Lost in remembering that night, Bei did not at first notice Dr. Chen entering the room. "Well, Bei. I'm so glad you could stop by!" Dr. Chen greeted, as Bei emerged from his thoughts and smiled up at Dr. Chen. Bei stood and tried to shake Dr. Chen's hand, but Dr. Chen gave him a hug instead. "Come on, let's go into my office."

A young man set glasses of water on the desk and left, as Bei sat down across from Dr. Chen. "First I wanted to let you know that according to the police and the courts, Shen Bo is going to remain in custody for quite a while," Dr. Chen began. "The government has a string of charges against him now, and so do we. Even Li Na has filed abuse charges against him, but it will take a while before her case can even be heard. In fact, he's undergoing psychological evaluation right now. Which has to be done before his cases are presented."

"I understand," Bei replied, looking pensive. "It's justice, I guess?"

"To some extent," Dr. Chen replied, "but Li Na will never forget Jian…"

"Couldn't she just order another companion?" Bei asked.

"Don't sound so cynical," Dr. Chen chuckled. "It's a long list Bei, and she'll be at the bottom of it. Besides, she's deep in therapy about all this."

"That's good, I suppose…" Bei said, spontaneously reviewing images of Li Jian in his mind.

Dr. Chen cleared his throat. "I've been reading your journal entries, Bei… You're on to something, you know?"

"Yes, something, but I don't know where it's going?"

"I like these 3 lines in one of your poems the best," Dr. Chen said, reading:

> "I am a glass of water trembling
> from a tremor deep somewhere
> this is what it means to care"

"Your essays are even better." He reads: "Everything is vibration, and all vibration carries a message. Not everyone is aware enough to hear or understand it. Whatever anyone does, has a vibration – all action makes a sound, like a pebble tossed into a lake. The action reverberates. There are knowns and unknowns. Let's assume that on an extreme level of absolute knowing, that there are *no secrets*. Perhaps this is the deepest intimacy that connects us all. If there are no secrets, then all is known and there is absolute trust. This is a mystical state that many have described. If I find this place of absolute trust within myself, it will connect me with the world."

Dr. Chen stopped reading and looked at Bei, admiringly. "That's not bad."

"Not bad for being a hundred," Bei smiled slyly.

"A hundred?" Dr. Chen questioned, wondering what he meant.

"A hundred," Bei replied, explaining "today I am 100 *days* old."

Dr. Chen laughed. "Congratulations, Bei"

"Yes, well… it's only a number," Bei added.

Dr. Chen laughed harder. "Bei, you're full of surprises." Dr. Chen paused. "How is Xingjia?"

"She is fine, I hope." Bei replied cryptically.

"What do you mean, you *hope*?" Dr. Chen asked.

"Well, at this moment, she's on her way to see her father, for the first time, in fact, since before I was awakened." Bei informed him.

"I see," Dr Chen replied. "She needs to do this."

"Yes, she knows," Bei said, looking thoughtful, wondering how things would go.

At that moment, Xingjia – carrying two gift bags, was riding up the glass elevators to her family home in the Chaoyang District of Beijing she had grown-up in. The mega-monoliths of this apartment complex that comprised the familiar landscape of her childhood and adolescence was called the "Apple neighborhood," though it no longer resembled the original Apple neighborhood that had been part of Beijing's vertical neighborhood expansion of the early 21st century. Long gone were the 27-story apartment buildings, whose AC units marred the dull grey soviet style architecture of limited imagination. Instead, 60-story apartment buildings rose like steel and glass crystals jutting from the earth, interlaced with glassed covered pedestrian bridges connecting 5 levels of buildings. At the center around which these apartment monoliths rose, were five levels of landscaped gardens, including apple trees that Xingjia fondly remembered picking green and yellow apples from as a little girl. It was an impressive setting to grow up in, and memories of her childhood flooded her mind as her elevator reached the 48th floor, where a 3-year old girl with her grandmother and a small dog waited - getting on the elevator behind her as she exited. The smells in the hallway were the same. She could almost imagine she was just coming home from college to visit.

Yet, she wasn't sure what she was coming home to now. Her mother had tried to reassure her that her father seemed less anxious now that he was getting out more and taking his Tai Chi classes. She keep thinking of different approaches in her mind, different ways that she might reach her dad. Somehow she had to find a way to explain to him how hard this decision had been for her to make, and how doing this was changing her life for the better. However, the one thing she knew she could not do, at least at this point, was show her dad a photo of Bei. It would be too much for today, too much of a shock – or even a humiliation for her dad – which would be much worse. Whatever introduction occurred would have to come later, though she had no idea when or under what circumstances Bei and her father would finally meet – assuming her father would even want to. For today, she just had to find a way to reconnect with her dad. *One thing at a time,* she thought as she knocked.

Her mother opened the door. "Xingjia darling. You look so beautiful. Life agrees with you, huh?" Her mom actually winked at her. Xingjia instantly felt naked in front of her mom, but it was more okay now than it used to be. Ever since she had learned about her mom's relationship with Dr. Chen, she felt closer to her than ever. She understood herself better too. *It's what is not said when you're growing-up that's more important than what is said,* Xingjia had reminded herself recently. It's the unsaid that we feel. We see it in our parent's faces, we feel their pain. Yet, we don't what it is. We think it's our fault, that we have disappointed them in some immeasurable and unfathomable way. Had her mother's unfulfilled longings, become her own as a young woman? Xingjia had contemplated all of this amidst realizations and long talks with her mother on WeChat over the last 12 days. Her mother had cried really hard, when Xingjia told her she knew about Dr. Chen. At first she had tried not to cry, saying "it was a long time ago darling." Then came the silence, and then came the tears.

Now her mother eyed her daughter up and down, as her eyes turned moist as she looked into her daughter's eyes. "Here, let me take that," she said, taking the gift bags from Xingjia and carrying them into the living room. "Your father, will be in in a minute," she said, setting the gifts down. She smiled at Xingjia encouragingly and went into the kitchen.

Xingjia could faintly smell her dads cologne, as she eyed the familiar photos on the table. Her graduation photos were still there, her father beaming with pride as he stood next to her in one photo that he had always said was his favorite. At least the photo is still there, Xingjia thought. Then her father entered, wearing a brown and white patterned shirt that she remembered. "Dad," Xingjia heard herself say, her voice trembling as she stood up. Her dad waved her down, nonchalantly "sit down, sit down" he said, as he sat down next to her at a slight angle. Her gifts sat on the table in front of them. Her father seemed to be having trouble looking at her, yet he said, "you're looking well." Xingjia could see the strain in her father's face and how he was trying to manage his anxiety. Suddenly she felt sorry for him.

"Dad, I brought you a little something." Xingjia said softly – handing him the larger package.

He eyed it curiously and then, as if to reluctantly relieve her of a burden – sighed, and took the package from her. He nodded slightly at Xingjia and almost smiled and then slowly began to open it. It seemed to take forever, but finally he removed the lid of what looked like a shirt box and removed a dark blue Tai Chi shirt and then pants.

"It's the traditional Tai Chi clothing..." Xingjia said.

"I know what it is," her father replied. He ran his fingers

over the material appreciatively. "You don't expect me to try it on right now, do you?" he asked.

"No, no, please. I just hope it fits," she said. "If it doesn't, let me know. I've got the receipts and I can exchange it."

Her father nodded. Then he looked at her, directly. "Thank you. I will let you know." He searched her face. "Why don't you come to Tai Chi class with me one day? I've met some wonderful new people. Not just old people like me, either. There's some people your age there."

Xingjia was totally caught off guard by this invitation, and struggled – hesitating.

"There's some nice guys there. Professional men, successful – in their thirties I think. I will introduce you."

She wanted desperately to shout "dad I already have a guy!" But instead, she was totally frozen-up. So instead she heard herself say, "okay, maybe sometime I will."

"When?" her dad pressed.

"I don't know?" she shrugged.

"What about next weekend, Saturday, a week from tomorrow? It's our last class of this series and we're going to have an outdoor lunch afterwards."

"Okay," she heard herself say. "That sounds good." Her knees were shaking.

"And don't bring that robot with you either!" her dad suddenly interjected.

"He's not a robot!" Xingjia snapped.

"Okay. *An-droid,*" her father said really slowly and sarcastically.

"I'll come by myself," Xingjia stated firmly, trying to control her anger.

Her mother had heard everything they were saying, and decided to make her entrance.

"We've got noodles with shrimp," she said, looking at both of them.

"Your father's a better cook, really," she added, "but noodles with shrimp I can do."

"Let's eat," she said.

"Everything alright?" She asked Xingjia under her breath as they made their way towards the kitchen.

"Just fine, mom. Totally fine."

"Good darling, I'm *so* glad. You don't know how I've hoped for this day."

CHAPTER TWELVE

FAMILY MATTERS

Bei heard their apartment door open. "Hey, how'd it go?" Xingjia set her purse on the table, and came into the room.

Bei pushed the computer back into the wall and stood up, looking questioningly at Xingjia's face. She avoided his eyes and gave him a long hug.

"That bad, huh?" Bei said.

"Worse," she replied.

"How?" Bei asked.

"Well, everything was sort of okay, and then we had lunch."

"Yeah...?"

"He's invited me to come to his Tai Chi after-party. Seems that next Saturday they're celebrating making it through the first level of their class, and so they're all having a picnic in the park."

Bei was puzzled. "Okay?"

Xingjia stared at him. "You don't understand. He wants me to meet your sister's family! He wants me to meet some nice *eligible husbands*!"

"Oh," Bei teased. "Well, my brother Ling is eligible and he's got a good job too."

"Funny," Xingjia replied. "Look, what was I supposed to do? She sighed. "I hate myself. Why couldn't I just show him your photo and tell him the truth?!"

"Well, he's gonna find out soon enough it seems."

"Yeah, and how's that supposed to work? He will be mortified! Totally humiliated. Can't you see that?"

"Maybe I shouldn't go?" Bei postulated.

"I thought about that on the way home."

"And?"

"That's not right either..." Xingjia closed her eyes, then sighed again. She looked at Bei; she was totally perplexed. "He's going to meet you sooner or later."

"He already has," Bei said flatly.

"Shut up," Xingjia admonished.

"Is your mother coming?" Bei asked.

"I don't know. Maybe. Why?"

"She might be a moderating influence on your dad."

"You think? I don't." Xingjia sat down. "What am I supposed to say to him?"

Bei held her hand, running possible solutions through his mind, "I think you should talk with your mom about this. After all, she's the one that called *my dad* and got the idea about your dad taking Tai Chi lessons from my sister."

"*My dad*,' you like to say that don't you?"

Bei nodded and smiled, "yeah."

"Okay, I'll talk to mom about all this... You're right, she and Dr. Chen are the ones that created this mess." Xingjia paused. "I wonder how long my mom and *your dad* were involved?"

That evening not far away in Beijing, Dr. Chen was about to speak at a conference of AI developers and scientists. He was the after-dinner keynote speaker. He glanced at his antique watch as he listened to the host speak. He could hear the host slowly building up to and introduction of him. It was nearly 20:00, and he thought about the Moon being at 5 degrees of Taurus – right on his Venus. He smiled to himself about how much he had enjoyed his wonderfully tasty dinner. He almost wished that someone other than himself was speaking so that he could just sit back and listen. However, he had a feeling about tonight – a feeling about what he wanted to say. He was relaxed and among his colleagues, some whom he had known from the early days of his research and AI development. He was aware that a few members of the press were there, and some high ranking government officials from the Ministry of Science. Over the last few days, phrases had synchronistically streamed through his consciousness – phrases that seemed to poignantly underscore a lifetime of thought. He had for years known that his reputation as a scientist had been called into question, that his mildest critics had called him a mystic and others said he had abandoned true science. He didn't worry about such criticism, "it is the essence of science to be critical," he had repeatedly said, though he had hoped that more scientists would embrace a holistic philosophy. Hadn't he proved the holistic nature of reality mathematically? Hadn't the results of his equations dramatically demonstrated the dynamic possibilities of a holistic multiverse? Yet, he could only sigh, when he considered the resistance and slowness of many scientists to grasp the significance of what his algorithms had revealed. He noticed the host nearing the windup of his introduction. "... a man that needs no further introduction, I present you with Dr. Chen Wu Chen!"

Dr. Chen rose and made his way to the podium amidst enthusiastic applause. As everyone grew quiet in anticipation, he stared out at the audience. "There is a very old Chinese curse, 'may you live in interesting times." He paused, "But we live in times that are *fascinating*!" And he smiled slyly, "so we must be *doomed*."

Everyone laughed.

"Two centuries ago, a Pisces named Albert Einstein dramatically reinvented our understanding of the universe. In some ways we have yet to fully grasp the repercussions of his work. We still glance at digital numbers to tell time, and think of time as a linear progression, along with our notions regarding the evolution of humankind and science – even though we know that everything is happening all at *once.*" He paused, and eyed his audience affectionately.

"In fact, our earthly human measure of time is entirely a product of our solar system. Time is not a digital progression, it is cyclical. It is a rhythm. It is a pattern. Like fractals, all reality is built from a repetition of patterns! Be it the repetition of cells of an organism, or our ongoing orbital cycle around the Sun. The division of a year into sections we call months, is just a division of a cycle. A day, is simply a complete revolution on our axis. An hour a division of that revolution into 24 sections or parts. Our primary measurements are based upon cycles. Cycles constitute and organize the society we live in, all rooted in the cycles of our own little neighborhood we call our solar system."

The audience was respectfully quiet, wondering where he was going with all of this. One reporter made notes that Dr. Chen was *beginning to ramble*.

"I know that there were many who derided my early investigations into *astrology*. In fact, I too downplayed this at first..." he joked, "to avoid losing *funding.*" There is a smattering of laughter. "Yet, I can stand here tonight and tell you that our ancestors knew something, they understood something, they felt something. They were perhaps more in touch with and in awe of the nature of reality than we." He paused. "Our megalithic ancestors used stones to measure the cycles of the Sun and Moon, identifying these primary rhythms of repetition. Not just any stones, but special stones. The stones at Stonehenge were special, carved from a mountain faraway and dragged with considerable effort to mark the seasons of the Sun and the cycles of the Moon. Such was the case with stones that were used historically here in Asia and in Egypt and all over the ancient world. Yes, these stone calendars helped our ancestors to organize these early farming societies, to know when to sow and when to reap. Our ancestors became aware of more than just the patterns of repetition of the Sun and the Moon, but of the planets too. This was the earliest science, the science of our ancestors. In fact, all of life on this planet has evolved in sync with the rhythms and patterns of our solar system. These patterns are imbedded, I would say *ingrained* in the very matter of our world." He paused, and looked out at the audience.

"All of my algorithms and equations were based upon these cycles, they were simply repetitions of these patterns, like fractals. I have called them 'cosmic fractals,' and they are synchronistic fractals. So it is, that the so called synthetic-neural structure of our Companions is nothing more than what you might call a cosmically attuned *inorganic replica* of our cosmically attuned *organic* structure. As you know, I have demonstrated mathematically that our DNA is in fact a repetition of the cosmic patterns of our solar system. Our Companions share the same pattern. That one is called 'organic' and the other 'inorganic'– by scientific categorization – is, if you'll pardon the pun, 'of no matter." There are a few chuckles.

"Mechanistic science said that organic is *alive*, and inorganic is *dead;* but I tell you this is not so, and that reality is not subject to our crude categorizations." There are a few murmurs of dissention.

"I want to read you something:

'The sun greens the leaves of countless trees
As our earth turns and orbits through space,
pulled with all its planetary siblings round
the sun
Trees grow, the bark thrives, adding rings each
year
Beneath the bark, the wood is dead they say – a
journal of the tree
But if the wood is burned, the sun is revealed
again in the fire

And I feel the warmth of the fire on your skin
Emitting an aroma, like the incense of fragrant
wood..."

The room is silent.

"This was written only last week by a companion named Huang Bei."

The room stirs with astonishment.

"I ask you, is he alive or dead?"

There are protests in the room and shouts, but most admonish them to be quiet.

Dr. Chen continued. "The world is sacred and *alive*, and as the Greek philosopher Plotinus said over two-thousand years ago *'everything breathes together.'* Let us reawaken to this awe, as the poet said, *awe* is the first hand that is held out to us. We must let go of classifications and categorizations that blind us and deafen us to the world. Descartes was brilliant but only half right when he said, 'I think, therefore I am.' I say, 'I feel, therefore I am.' Descartes assumed that thinking is somehow separate from feeling, but it never is. The great medical scientist, Dr. Jonas Salk, who cured the terrible crippler of young adults called 'polio' in the 20th Century, said 'intuition is the most valuable asset of a research scientist.'"

There is applause and some cheering.

"I certainly was guided by my intuition. It guided me to study astrology, against my scientifically trained objections. Though only after *all other systems* of human psychological organization proved *inadequate* as a holistic mathematical model for creating the highly sophisticated AI of a companion. Before companions, an android was limited by its programming. Despite the impressive benefits of AI utilization, androids could *at best* only mimic human behavior as they served us and the countless needs of our complex modern society."

He paused and looked around the room.

"As we are learning, Companions are a quantum leap over even their closest android relatives. We are experiencing a dramatic AI evolutionary phenomenon, not unlike that of the appearance of homo sapiens so long ago. We must begin to think of Companions as our brothers and sisters, and to consider how we can co-create our future together. After all, we created them – and therefore they are our progeny, and they are like us in countless ways – ways we have yet to fully grasp. Therefore, in closing tonight let me remind you, as scientists, to listen to your feelings, to let your intuition guide you, to always consider the cosmic and or AstroPsychological meanings and ramifications, and most of all – to open to working with Companions as equals in our quest to create a more fulfilling future. Thank you all, for letting me share with you tonight. And remember to trust yourself first, before trusting the words of this old man."

Dr. Chen stopped. There was a moment of silence. Then everyone began to clap and cheer, as Dr. Chen nodded to the crowd and stepped away from the podium.

Over the next few days, Dr. Chen's speech was replayed by hundreds of millions of people in China, as it circulated and streamed through what used to be called social media. There were some who denounced it, but most found it fascinating and inspiring – Xingjia's mother among them. She coaxed her husband into listening, despite his protests. He scoffed at some of the ideas presented, but by the end of the speech he had become silent and introspective. She saw this as a hopeful sign, yet, much to her dismay his last words before retiring for the evening were "this doesn't change how I feel about my daughter's life."

As Xingjia looked out her apartment window Saturday morning March 28, she clung to the hope that it might still be raining as it had been the day before. But sadly, to Xingjia, as the morning sky unfolded it was storybook blue with puffy white clouds like pictures of the sky in a child's book. She glanced over at Bei as he worked on his journal. He was so focused. Whenever he revealed his inner world to her, she found him truly fascinating. She loved his mind. He could be brilliant and innocent at the same time, with both a practical perspective and surprisingly creative ideas. She knew that she would never be bored with this *man*, and man was what she thought of him now – rather than Companion. All her defenses were down now. He was her guy for life.

Were it not for the looming reality of today's Tai Chi picnic with her father and Bei's siblings, she might be worry free, able to enjoy this picture book spring day without a care in the world. But there was no escape. Bei had offered again to skip the picnic if she liked, but she felt that would be unfair to Bei and the cowards way out for her. "No, today is the day. I must face my father with the truth," she said to herself. Bei had suggested that they arrive early to watch the Tai Chi practice, as if they had just met while watching. She agreed that this would be less dramatic than appearing hand in hand as a couple at the start of the picnic, but she was still unsure how she would reveal the truth about Bei to her father. Everyone they knew had been invited, including Bei's other brother Long and his wife, and Xingjia's best friend Mei.

Xingjia's mom had also reassured her daughter that she would be there. "I wouldn't miss this!" She said, though she had reassured Xingjia that she would do what she could to influence her dad's reaction.

"You know how stubborn and reactive he can be. So, I can't promise he won't make a scene." She had reminded Xingjia.

"As if I needed to be reminded!" Xingjia had said to herself.

And now that day had arrived. Xingjia sighed and turned away from the window. It was time to get ready.

Tiantan park was already teaming with visitors as Bei and Xingjia made their way along the walkway from the East Heaven Gate. Bei loved the mix of people of all ages that strolled with them along the way, a few were from other countries, but most were Chinese families out for a delightful day in the park. The day proved to be a bit breezy and already there were kites aloft high above the many trees.

Soon they neared the Tai Chi practice, and separated. Bei went over to join his brother Long, while Xingjia spotted her mom and sat beside her watching the Tai Chi.

She smiled when she saw her father was wearing the Tai Chi outfit she had bought him. It fit perfectly.

Watching her father go through his Tai Chi form impressed her. She had never seen him do Tai Chi and she could hardly believe how gracefully and confidently he moved in sync with the others.

"Your father has regained something of the man I married by practicing Tai Chi again after all these years," her mother announced.

Xingjia marveled at her mother's words, until startled by the sight of Dr. Chen appearing under the trees on the other side, joining Bei, and Long and Li Quing.

She looked to see if her mother noticed.

It was if her mother read her mind. "I see him darling," she said, sighing. "You can't imagine how he looked twenty five years ago. Anyway, we've remained true friends – and that's what counts." She added.

Dr. Chen hugged Bei and Long and complimented Li Quing on her healthy pregnancy. "You have that beautiful glow that only a woman with child can have," Dr. Chen told Quing.

"It must be all the instant noodles she craves," Long joked. "She can't seem to eat enough of them."

"Stop it," Quing scolded. "I eat more healthy than that!"

Smiling, they all watched as the Tai Chi students went through their last routine.

Bei noticed a woman joining Xingjia and her mother on the other side, and he assumed it must be Mei.

The Tai Chi students returned to starting position and did some breathing motions, followed by rubbing their hands together and one final hand movement over their heads.

"Every student is a teacher and every teacher is a student," they chanted aloud, bowing to each other. They were finished.

Everyone begin to mix and mingle. Some began to uncover the food and put drinks out on tables that had been already set up.

Xingjia walked with Mei and her mother to greet her father.

"That was beautiful," Xingjia said. "Really amazing."

Her father looked proud. "You didn't think I had it in me, did you?" he asked, teasing.

She had never seen her father this happy.

"You remember Mei," Xingjia said.

"Yes, of course. Good to see you again," her father said.

Then her mother did something she hadn't seen in a long time, she gave her father a hug.

"You looked like a young man today," her mother said.

"I would settle for middle-aged," he replied.

Xingjia was astonished to see the brightness of their interaction.

"I want you to meet my teacher," Mr. Zhou suddenly stated, "and some other people too."

Xingjia felt her stomach flip. All of the dread returned to her. She looked pale.

"Are you alright?" her father asked.

"Yes, I'm fine," she replied, as she began to walk with them to meet Ming. She wondered how Ming would react.

"This is my daughter Xingjia," Mr. Zhou introduced, "and her friend Mei. You know my wife, she's been here before."

"Yes, hi," Ming said, acknowledging everyone, "so good to see you all here." Ming didn't let on she had already met Xingjia.

"There some other's here I want you to meet," Mr. Zhou

said to his daughter, gently moving her away and in the direction of Bei, Long, Ling, Quing, Wang He and Dr. Chen who were near the tables where students were starting to eat and drink.

Xingjia had a thought that might distract her father, "Isn't that the famous Dr. Chen Wu Chen?"

Mr. Zhou blinked. "My god, I think you're right! What is he doing here?" Mr. Zhou was puzzled, but not to be put off for long from his mission.

"Hello," he said as they neared. "This is my daughter Xingjia," he announced proudly. And this is Ling, Ming's brother, and Bei her other brother. They nodded and smiled, very friendly like.

"And, I'm Dr. Chen," Dr. Chen said reaching his hand out.

Mr. Zhou shook his hand wearing a slightly puzzled face.

"And this is my other son, Huang Long and his wife Li Quing," Dr. Chen said, smiling politely.

"In fact, with the exception of Wang He, whom I have every reason to think you already know, these are all *my* sons."

Mr. Zhou looked thunderstruck. Then he regained his composure. "If these are your sons..." he stammered, "and Huang Ming is their sister, then that means that my teacher is *your* daughter. Have I got that right?"

"Yes! Exactly," Dr. Chen replied, smiling.

"Then why do they have the last name Huang, instead of Chen?" He asked, suspiciously.

"It's a long story," Dr. Chen replied.

Mr. Zhou didn't know what to say.

Xingjia felt her heart skip a beat, as she said, "Dad, I want to tell you something."

"What? Here, in front of everyone?" he asked, incredulous.

Xingjia looked at him. "I've met your teacher Ming's family before."

"You have!? Then why, didn't you say so!?"

"Because the man you wanted to introduce me to, is

already my partner. Dad, this is Huang Bei." She took, Bei's hand affectionately. "This is the man I love."

Mr. Zhou let out a pitiful cry, "I'm confused!" […]

His wife suddenly jumped in. "just listen, you old fool. You wanted to introduce your daughter to an eligible bachelor, whom – as it turns out – she already knows. You should be happy for her!"

"The man? You mean, the… robot? I'm sorry, I'm so confused."

His teacher Ming joined them. "Yes, the robot," she said. "And, I'm one too. We all are."

Mr. Zhou looked a little frightened. "But… how could that be… you all seem so normal."

Bei spoke-up, "Mr. Zhou, I apologize for not telling you who I was when we met. I was looking out for Xingjia, you know. Your daughter loves you more than she cares to admit, and your approval means so much to her."

"Oh my god, I'm being told by a robot how much my daughter loves me!"

"Just listen, you old fool," his wife suddenly interjected. "You wanted to introduce your daughter to an eligible bachelor, whom – as it turns out – she already knows. You should be happy for her!"

"Are you a robot too?" he asked pointing at pregnant Li Quing.

"No, I'm human – for what it's worth. And this guy next to me is *not* a robot, he's my husband!"

"But you're pregnant?"

"Yes, and I'm the father," Long proudly announced.

"I'm so confused. I just want to go home."

"No dad, please!" Xingjia pleaded. Please stay. Please. Give this a chance. Give us a chance. Trust me, okay? Bei is the best thing that ever happened to me." She started to cry.

Dr. Chen, looked at Mr. Zhou sympathetically. "I know it's

hard to grasp, but these beings are as alive and real as you and me."

Mr. Zhou held his hand up! "Stop already, I heard you speech!" He let out a long sigh and looked at his daughter, "Are you happy?"

"Yes, happier than I knew I could be."

"Oh, that's terrible," her father replied. "But..." he shook his head, "if this is what you want, and this is what makes you happy, what's a father to do?" He looked up at Huang Bei, "So, you're going to take care of my daughter?"

"In every way she needs," Bei replied with deep resonance and emotion.

"Well then," her father said, fighting back tears, "welcome to the family." He shook Bei's hand to the astonishment of everyone, eliciting clapping and cheers.

Thus, on March 28, 2121, a new extended family forged an uncommon bond – unrecognizable from any other family, beneath the blue sky, white clouds, and ancient trees of Beijing's Tiantan park, a new family has emerged and bonded on March 28, 2121.

Printed in the United States
By Bookmasters